HOLIDAY BRIDAL WAVE

GWYN MCNAMEE
CHRISTY ANDERSON

Holiday Bridal Wave

© 2020 Gwyn McNamee & Christy Anderson

To the hopeless romantics who believe in holiday miracles, this one is for you!

ACKNOWLEDGMENTS

We love writing the Warren family! Thank you to all the beta readers and all those who have helped share their love of *Holiday Bridal Wave.* We appreciate your support more than we can ever say.

CHAPTER 1

ARCHIMEDES

"**I**s this some kind of fucking joke?"

It has to be. There's no way this is real.

Mother slams her palm against the table, rattling the fine china holding the Thanksgiving feast we've just finished eating. "Archimedes Warren! Language!"

Father just scowls at me from his position at the opposing end of the long, ornate table. One of his dark eyebrows rises slowly, a patented look that screams his displeasure. "Am I laughing? No, it's not a joke."

I seek out the only person who might still retain any semblance of sanity in this family. But Grandmother offers nothing but a sympathetic look from her spot across the table from me.

Oh, my God!

My hand holding the stack of papers quivers with my anger. "Did you two know about this?"

I should have expected this from Grandfather but not her. Never her. Not after the way she stood up for Artemis when he decided to leave the company. Not after she went to bat for him and Pen when Mom and Dad wanted to completely disown him for marrying her.

And to drop this on me now?

It's Thanksgiving. Five weeks until New Year's Eve.

Five. Weeks.

I shake the offending document toward Grandfather and then the man who sired me. "You can't be serious about this."

Father simply glares at me from the head of the table. "I'm dead serious, son."

"But—" I squeeze my eyes shut and scrub my free hand over my face, "that means I can only take over as CEO if I'm married by December 31st."

An oppressive silence settles over the room. The holidays can always be stifling with the Warrens, but this is a whole new level of soul-crushing—even for us. This is going above and beyond the typical meddling and overbearing involvement in their children's lives. This is just…cruel.

But Father doesn't even blink, just stares back at me with the frosty blue eyes he gave each of us. "That's exactly what it means."

"That's five fucking weeks from now!"

Mother lurches to her feet, both hands smacking the table so hard, red wine sloshes over the side of her crystal glass and onto the off-white silk tablecloth. "*Archimedes Leonidas Warren*! You *will* watch your language at my table. I don't care if you're an adult now. I'm still your mother, and you still owe me some damn respect."

I have to bite my tongue not to point out the fact that she just swore, too, as I crumple the trust papers into a tight ball.

Father snorts and glances at my hand. "That's not the original, son. You can't destroy it and expect this all to go away."

2

Athena surveys everyone at the table. She's been unusually quiet thus far, probably saving up to dish out something that will send Mom and Dad over the edge—as is typical for my little sis. "So…" she picks up her wine glass and twirls in between her fingers, "is anyone going to clue me in on what's going on?"

I still can't believe Mom and Dad let her drink before she's twenty-one. Artie and I never would've gotten away with that. Then again, I think they're just so sick of trying—and failing—to make her stop doing *anything* that they're willing to let her practically get away with murder for fear of losing her the way they "lost" Artie.

If this isn't the last straw in showing her the type of people Mom and Dad really are, then I don't know what would be.

I let out a mirthless laugh and shake my head. "Well, dear sister, Mother and Father, and it seems Grandfather and Grandmother, have seen fit to amend the family trust."

Her eyes widen slightly. "Oh?"

"Yes." I allow my gaze to linger on Grandmother again, hoping she'll speak up against this atrocity, but it appears that despite her previous attempts to smooth things over and try to keep this family from tearing itself apart, she's staying mute on this subject. I uncrumple the ball of paper and find the relevant paragraph. "*In order to acquire and maintain the position of CEO at Warren Enterprises Worldwide, said individual must be legally married—consummated and legitimate, not just in name—which shall mean residing with his or her spouse for at least 330 days a year...* Oh, and this is the best part...*with the expectation of an heir within one year of said marriage.* Which means, if I ever get divorced, or they find out it's a sham, and if I don't impregnate my *loving* wife almost immediately, I end up on my ass and kicked out of the family business without a fucking penny."

Athena chokes on her wine and finally manages to swallow it. "Well, shit."

Mother growls. "Not you, too."

"Sorry, Mom." Athena's shoulders rise and fall nonchalantly. "But that's kind of bullshit."

This time, Father slams his fist against the table so hard it rattles the glasses. "That's enough out of you two. Grandfather and I did what we had to do to protect the family. After your brother ran off with that harlot and their bastard child, we needed to do something to ensure that the family business is going to move forward with a Warren at the helm, one who is a dedicated family man and not prone to scandal or running off whenever his dick twitches."

Athena snorts and covers her mouth with her hand as she looks at me. "Dad, if you think that's not gonna happen with Archimedes then—"

"Shut it, little sister."

I've had my fair share of romantic dalliances in the past, but I'm discreet about it. I know better than to tarnish the Warren name with illicit affairs. Artie was young when he met Penelope. Young and too dumb to realize what his actions then would lead to now. I don't think I've ever been as pissed at him in my life as I am at this moment. This is because of Artie. The man is blissfully happy and has everything he's ever dreamed of, but in order to get it, he left me in this quagmire.

He never wanted the company. He never wanted the power. It's all I've ever wanted, and now, I'm not going to be able to get it because these requirements are absolutely ludicrous. It's almost as if they *want* me to fail. But that makes no sense. That would only leave Athena to take over, and she would need to comply with this ridiculous requirement, too. She's still in college. And she's more than demonstrated her contempt for the company. Enough that I don't think any of us expect her to come home to work when she graduates. That will never happen, and they know it, which means they fully expect me to comply with the trust and find a wife in little more than a month.

Absolute insanity!

I suck in a deep, fortifying breath, trying to regain some semblance of control. Perhaps there's an opportunity to approach this diplomatically, to come to some sort of middle-ground on these requirements. "Why the deadline, Father? That gives me what...thirty-seven days to get married?"

He plasters on the fake Warren smile, the one we've all practiced so well and polished to perfection. "From what I hear, you have a lot of very lovely lady friends. It shouldn't be hard to find one willing to commit their life to you, given the billions of dollars you stand to inherit." He shrugs. "Pick one."

Pick one?

He cannot be fucking serious.

Not one of the women I choose to spend my nights with is anyone I would choose to spend my *life* with. And he knows it.

This is a punishment. I'm being punished because Artemis couldn't keep his dick in his pants when he was eighteen. I don't have any unplanned children running around—at least, not that I know of—yet, I'm the one who's now going to have to figure out a way around this trust provision in the next five weeks.

If Artie were here right now, he'd be getting a swift kick to the face or better yet...the cock...since that's what got him in so much trouble in the first place. I fucking love the guy. And Penelope. And Max. But Christ...has he put me in a position.

I drop the crumpled paper on my empty dinner plate and

shove back my chair from the table. All eyes follow me as I rise to my feet. I button my suit coat and meet the eyes of everyone at the table before finally landing on Father. "I don't know what you thought this would accomplish. But if you want to keep a Warren at the helm, this isn't the way to do it. What if I'm not able to comply with the terms in the next five weeks?"

Father shrugs again, but I know it's a major pressing question. His eyes flick over to Athena. "There's always your sister."

And I'm sure he has something up his sleeve to force her into compliance, too.

BLAIRE

The elevator pings, announcing his arrival. But I've known he was coming ever since Rinaldo down at security called up to give me the warning that Archimedes had entered the building and that he'll be blowing in like a hurricane.

You would think the nice, long holiday weekend would have relaxed Archimedes a little bit, but as soon as those elevator doors open, he storms in, tosses his jacket at me, and barrels past my desk into his office.

The glass door swings shut behind him, and he slams his briefcase on top of the desk so loudly it reverberates through his office and even hurts my ears out here.

I cringe and stand to hang his coat in the small closet to the left of my desk.

It's freezing out there this Monday morning. With winter finally descending on New York, big, fat snowflakes fall outside the floor-to-ceiling windows and blanket Central Park just beyond them.

It's absolutely beautiful.

My favorite time of the year, the time when holiday joy spreads through the city and miracles can happen. Even though Mom died before I ever really got to know her, the memories of wonderful holidays spent with Dad still live on in my heart. The years since he's been gone haven't been easy, but having good friends with warm, open arms during the season and the overall cheer in the air helps me make it through.

I glance down at the two dozen Christmas-themed snow globes covering my desk and sigh. So pretty. So relaxing. So…crisp and clean. Like the world is waking to a fresh start and new beginning with every snowfall.

But not everyone loves the season the way I do, and if you hate it, it sure makes it a bitch when you have to go outside during a snowstorm.

Maybe the weather is what has Archimedes in such a shit mood.

It's the only obvious reason. He had really been looking forward to the weekend. A few days away with one of his bed-buddy bunnies after Thanksgiving dinner with his family.

Vermont for skiing, if I remember correctly.

Or maybe it was Connecticut?

I scan my calendar notes. Vermont. That's right— Connecticut is the upcoming Christmas vacation with bed bunny number two. Sometimes, it's hard to keep them straight. The man goes through women the way most people do clean underwear.

"Blaire! Get in here!" Archimedes' bellow reaches me even through his closed door, and I cringe once more.

So much for a nice, relaxing, post-holiday Monday workday.

I grab a notepad off my desk and make my way to his office. Even with the door shut, I can hear him mumbling to himself as he paces back and forth.

Archimedes doesn't pace. Nor does he mumble.

He's usually so put together. The perfect example of a Warren heir. Which is what he became after Artie essentially cut himself off from the family. When Archimedes Warren is in a mood, he rarely, if ever, shows it to anyone but me since I have an unfettered view of him in his glass-enclosed office. But he doesn't get rattled much. I don't think I've seen him like this more than three or four times in the year I've worked directly for him. It's why the warning from security before he came up was so surprising.

Something really serious must be going on.

My gut churns the white chocolate peppermint mocha I guzzled this morning on my way into work and threatens to bring it up my throat as I push open the door into his office. "You needed me, Mister Warren?"

His head snaps up, and cool blue eyes meet mine. With his broad, muscular shoulders pulled tight and his jaw clenched so hard, I can practically feel the tension in his body and his teeth threatening to crack.

Dammit. That shouldn't be so sexy.

The man is smoking hot as hell most days, but when he's angry, he's downright nuclear. The kind of heat that will burn you alive. It's no wonder he has zero trouble finding someone to warm his bed...whether it be in New York City, Vermont, Connecticut, or anywhere else in the world.

Those looks and this kind of money and power are a real aphrodisiac for women. *Other women.*

Because I *definitely* don't have a crush on my boss.

Nope. Definitely not at all.

That would be completely inappropriate. And I am always professional. My job means too much to me not to be. Yet, even after all this time, the fantasies of having him bend me over my desk and fuck me senseless still make an almost daily appearance—despite doing my best to keep them at bay.

It might be easier to control if I were getting any, but aside from an upcoming blind date, my love-life calendar has been as empty as Santa's sack at the end of Christmas night.

So, I'll just visualize this man doing nasty things to me and pray I don't slip up and make a comment that gets me fired for sexually harassing my boss.

Archie finally drags his focus away from me and drops into his large leather chair behind the massive hand-carved wood desk that takes up the vast majority of his office. "Shit. I'm sorry, Blaire. I didn't mean to yell at you."

I step in and offer my best *pleasant assistant here to help you with anything* smile. "No problem. Is something wrong, sir?"

He waves me off. "Please stop calling me *sir*. It makes me feel fucking old. And that's the last thing I want after this weekend. I'm twenty-five, for fuck's sake."

"What happened?"

It's none of my business. Not really. If it were something that affects the business this much, he would have called a swarm of lawyers and other employees—including me—to come into the office to work, even though we were on vacation. It can't be as bad as he's making it seem. Yet, Archimedes isn't one to overreact to anything...

His fists clench on the desktop, and he leans back in his chair and sighs. "My life got flipped upside down, that's what happened."

That doesn't sound good.

"Did something happen to your parents? Your grandparents? Artie or Athena?"

His family are the only people I can think of he's even remotely close enough with to react this way.

He lets out a long, slow sigh. "They're fine. Assholes, but fine."

Ouch.

Archimedes has never vocalized the Warren clan's

tension, but anyone with eyes can see it whenever they're in a room together. Last year's Christmas party was just...

Wow.

Between Artie getting stuck in that snowstorm and Athena getting drunk to avoid their grandmother, it was kind of a shitshow. And that's one thing Artemus and Bunny Warren do not tolerate. Neither is badmouthing the family. The fact that Archimedes is speaking so ill of them now means something truly awful happened.

"Is there anything I can help with, si—" I catch myself before the word fully forms, but his assessing gaze still narrows on me.

The corner of his mouth twitches. Almost like he's fighting a smile. "You can get me a cup of black coffee...and find me a wife."

CHAPTER 2

BLAIRE

"I'm sorry, Mister Warren isn't in the office at the moment. May I take a message?"

This phone has been ringing off the hook since I got in this morning—each call from a vapid heiress or starlet Archimedes has dated. News of his marriage predicament must have been leaked. It doesn't surprise me. Something this big is *huge* news in certain circles. It's like chum in shark-infested waters, and Archimedes is stuck and bleeding.

There isn't a woman in Manhattan or the greater state of New York who isn't going to throw their hat into the ring to be the bride of Archimedes Warren.

Who wouldn't want to marry a man who looks like that who is also worth billions?

I don't see much of a downside…except maybe having to deal with the Warren family for the rest of your life, or at least the rest of *theirs.*

Compared to his parents and grandparents, Archimedes is a dream. Which is why when he told me about the changes to the trust and his new predicament yesterday morning, I almost choked on my own breath. They are vile, evil, selfish people to thrust this upon him.

Though, a man like Archimedes Warren will have *no* problem finding a bride, even in such a short amount of time. A fact I offered to him immediately, to try to quell a little of his panic. He just looked at me with those eyes I could drown in and scrubbed his hands over his face before telling me it wasn't my problem and he wasn't going to involve me in his personal issues.

I figured he had a plan. I hadn't anticipated that plan to include calling a laundry list of exes who were exes for a reason.

The man is too damn smart for this.

He's not thinking clearly. It's the only explanation for why he would be willing to spend the rest of his life with any of these gold-digging snobs instead of someone he truly loves. He can't possibly want the company so much that he would risk being miserable for the next fifty years with someone he doesn't care about. Though, I'm not sure Archimedes even knows what love is, let alone whether he's ever *been* in love. He certainly hasn't been serious with anyone since I've worked here, and the way the tabloids paint the picture, the only thing Archimedes loves is being single.

The handsome devil himself strolls out of the elevator as I finish up the call and scribble out the fifteenth message before nine in the morning.

There's not enough coffee in the world for this day.

I grab my cup and take a sip of my white chocolate peppermint mocha while Archimedes chats with one of the corporate attorneys. You'd never know he has a handful of weeks to choose someone to be his wife. His passive, relaxed expression shows none of the pressure and stress he's under

—what I got a very rare glimpse of yesterday. Obviously, hiding your true feelings behind steely blue eyes is a Warren trait.

They are grace under fire. Perfection in an imperfect world.

I couldn't be more the opposite, dressed in my holiday apparel and tripping over my own words whenever I get nervous. He was born to be a leader, while I am much more comfortable following a step behind and offering assistance when needed. I prefer to stay *out* of the spotlight, when possible, while the Warrens seek it out and bask in it like they're flowers and it's the sun.

A long, slow sigh slips from my lips while ogling Archie. With his perfectly tailored suit molded to his lean, muscular body, he looks like he belongs on the cover of GQ more than in the boardroom, next in line to run one of the largest family-owned corporations in the world. That Italian silk pressed against his skin probably cost more than the trip to North Pole, Alaska, I've been saving up for the last two years.

It would be so easy to get bitter, seeing this kind of affluence flaunted every day, but Archimedes carries it so effortlessly. He's smug, but not in an *I want to punch him in the face* way. More like an *I want his cock to punch into my vagina* kind of way. He's difficult to work for, but not in an *I want to murder my boss and bury him in my rose garden* kind of way. More like an *I can't believe he's asking me to do this, but at least I'm getting paid overtime, and he appreciates my work* kind of way. And he's demanding, but not in a *my way or the highway* kind of way. More like a *bend over that desk so I can take you from behind, and I wouldn't hesitate for a second* kind of way.

I shift in my chair to ease some of the tension building between my legs. Working for Archimedes Warren can be a mixed blessing at times like these.

He smiles at something Chuck Jover says. Those little

creases that frame his eyes appear, and his Adam's apple bobs in the column of his tanned, muscled throat with his laughter. Entranced, I sip my drink and watch him like he's a reality show. Which, to be honest, he kind of is.

Lifestyles of the New York Rich and Ungodly Handsome...

The Warrens are basically American royalty. Their influence and reach know no bounds. They're like the Kennedys but with less scandal and more money. If Archimedes let someone film his search for a wife, it would be snatched up by one of the cable networks so fast, it would make his head spin. But he won't do that. He's much too *Warren* to invite that kind of salacious stuff into his life.

Which is precisely why these women...I glance down at the stack of messages for him...are all sorts of wrong. They're not the type of women he should be considering for a wife. Not at all.

Why can't he see that?

He says goodbye and turns my way. I take a final sip of coffee and set down my mug on its Christmas-themed warmer nestled between two of my favorite snow globes.

I stand and straighten my black-and-white-striped skirt, and he pauses next to my desk. He scans the Christmas items strewn across every available inch, including the two new globes I added this morning, and his lip twitches in amusement. His gaze briefly lands on my cardigan, where the elves are hard at work in various departments of Santa's workshop.

Since this is my first Christmas season working directly for Archimedes, he has yet to be exposed to my—shall we say—flamboyant exuberance for my favorite holiday. Though, he doesn't seem annoyed, which is good. I don't plan on changing how I celebrate just because he's a total Scrooge.

Mostly unfazed by my festive outfit and decor, he saunters past me, shoulders straight, head high, with the scent of rich leather and warm spice trailing in his wake.

I follow behind him and discretely inhale the heavenly smell assaulting me and sending a tingle through my entire body.

What the hell is he wearing? It smells so good.

But it's important to stay professional and get right to work instead of sniffing him. I flip through my notebook, ready to take notes at our daily morning meeting.

It's the routine we've fallen into since I got assigned to him. Every boss I've had during the years I've been with Warren Enterprises Worldwide—both as a student intern and then an employee since I graduated from community college—has been different in terms of what they expect. Archimedes expects perfection and accepts nothing less, yet somehow, I've managed to survive.

I shut the stylishly frosted-glass door and take a seat in front of his desk in one of the high-backed leather chairs.

The names of all the bimbos who have already called today stare up at me from the stack of messages. "You've had quite a few calls this morning already. Babette Lewis. Marilyn Martson. JoAnne Bellows and Marcella Morgan. Giselle Buchanan. Mirabella Owens…"

He sighs and leans back in his posh red-leather chair.

I glance up in time to see him grimace. "She said, and I quote, *'I know things ended poorly, but we always had chemistry where it counted. Happy to help a friend in his time of need. Call me.'*"

With a cringe, I rattle off the number. It ended very publicly and *very* badly for those two. Either she's hallucinating or so desperate to get him back that she's willing to pretend the bad stuff never happened.

As the Hollywood "it girl," acting is certainly in her repertoire, so I can see how that might make her an obvious choice. And when she and Archimedes dated, she had seemed totally smitten. The world ate them up. Too beautiful. Too powerful. Too wealthy.

And too good to be true.

The paparazzi caught the skank kissing her costar in her most recent film...offset. Archimedes dumped her faster than the speed of light. And their relationship wasn't the only thing that ended. So did her career—aside from an indie film every now and then. Needless to say, Warrens don't do scandals or second place, even in romance.

So, how in the world can he be considering marrying her?

I reach out to lay the number on his desk, with the stack of others I dropped there, but before I can set it down, he snatches it from my hand. The warm brush of his fingers against mine sends a shiver through my arm and straight to a place totally inappropriate for work. Not that it's unusual when I'm around Archimedes, but I try my best not to be affected by him.

Utter failure.

He balls up the note in his fist and raises his hand like he's going to throw it into the trash can, but he hesitates. With an annoyed sigh, he unfurls the note and places it on top of the stack. "Can't afford to rule anyone out right now, can I?"

Wait. What?

He pinches the bridge of his nose and leans back into his chair.

Before I can stop myself, my brain overrides my filter. "Mister Warren, you can't be serious? Mirabella Owens? After what she did to you, you'd still consider marrying her? Surely, you aren't that desperate?"

Shit.

I bite my bottom lip. I didn't mean to say that out loud. Especially that last part.

Did I really just call Archimedes Warren desperate?

He looks at me from over steepled fingers, one brow cocked before he leans forward, resting his crossed forearms on the desk. "You speak like you have knowledge on the subject. Please, do tell me why Mirabella is a bad choice. She's smart, beautiful, educated, good family. The perfect Warren bride. What more does one need?"

Love. But I don't say that. "Sir, if I may speak candidly?"

Humor flashes in his gaze, and a smirk tugs at his lips. "When are you not candid, Miss Hall?"

Crap. I guess I haven't been as professional in the past as I'd hoped.

He motions for me to continue.

I chew my lip for a moment. Then the words flow out of me like a river before I can second guess them. "Mirabella, while beautiful and talented, is a gold-digging attention whore."

ARCHIMEDES

Well, shit.

It looks like Miss Hall has more balls than I thought. Leave it to my quirky assistant to call it like it is. She doesn't always speak up, but when she does, it's always insightful and has proved invaluable in the past. And her observation about Mirabella is no different. I can't contain the laugh that bursts from my chest. "Yeah, she really is, isn't she?"

Blaire visibly relaxes and releases a nervous giggle while she holds her fingers up an inch apart to demonstrate her point. "Just a bit. And..." She shifts uncomfortably again and suddenly seems more interested in anything but looking at me. After a shaky breath, she meets my eyes again. "Sir, I hate to say this but...none of these girls," she waves a hand over the stack, "are any better. If they had been, wouldn't you still be with one of them?"

I narrow my gaze on her.

Maybe I've underestimated just how observant Miss Hall really is.

A deep sigh slips from my lips, and I sag back into my chair. "You're right." I shove a hand through my hair. "So, Miss Hall, what do I do, then? I have a handful of weeks to find a bride. Any suggestions?"

Because I sure as hell don't have any other ideas.

I've been wracking my brain since Thanksgiving dinner, and the ex-list was the only real plan I ever came up with. There are only so many ways to find a bride.

Her eyes brighten, sparkling at me—hopefully, because she has a brilliant plan. She squares her shoulders. "Mister Warren, I may have an idea."

This should be interesting.

I lean back in my chair and straighten my tie with one hand, my attention fixed on my very eccentric secretary. Blaire twists the gaudy plastic necklace lined with flashing Christmas bulbs between her fingers.

She's nervous. Whatever she's about to lay on me, it must be crazy. Like her. When she was first assigned to me, I almost refused—for several reasons. Her clothing is almost child-like—as if quirky and odd got together and created a fashion line just for her. Not exactly the image we want to present to people who come to meet with me at Warren Enterprises.

Today, it's the most God-awful sweater I have ever seen. Santa's workshop doesn't belong on a grown-ass woman. Neither do most of the things she wears—the patterned caricatured socks, the brightly printed dresses, the jewelry. It's only gotten worse the closer we've moved to the holiday season, too. First, it was the fall wardrobe, but once

November first hit, she went straight to Christmas and hasn't stopped going full force on the yuletide cheer, even though we've barely made it past Thanksgiving. Her obsession with all things Christmas might be a little intense, but I overlook it because Blaire Hall is as sharp as they come. Honestly, she could probably be the head of one of my departments, but she's been too valuable for me as an assistant to let her go.

Selfish? Yes, but necessary.

Everyone here loves her. Her kindness and compassion help compensate for my lack thereof. On top of that, she gets shit done. Plus, she's a great buffer between the other staff and me.

And despite her wardrobe choices, she isn't bad to look at, either. I would have to have been blind not to notice her the moment she walked in here. A delicate nose sits above perfectly pink soft lips, and a mass of curly red hair frames her pale, petite face.

One that's deepening into a dark shade of red. She isn't comfortable with this discussion. Neither am I—since I try my best to keep my private life just that—but it seems my comfort flew out the door the moment Grandfather signed the new trust documents.

Blaire may not want to get involved in my personal business, but her comment about Mirabella was spot-on. She was vapid, conceited, and more. The woman only cared about progressing her career, even at the expense of the man she claimed to love—me. I wasn't ready to pop the question or anything that extreme, but I definitely had some feelings for the woman, despite her negative traits. Thankfully, it was the one time the paparazzi's invasive behavior did me a favor by revealing her true nature.

And my lovely assistant was also right about the rest of the exes in this pile of messages. There isn't one of them I can really see myself spending the rest of my life with. That's a long fucking time to be stuck to someone, and these women were all temporary—though some may have lasted months instead of days or weeks—and they served a very specific purpose. They warmed my bed and were beautiful on my arm for events. These women appeased Mother and Father and let them believe I was getting serious about settling down, even though it couldn't have been further from the truth.

All I've ever wanted was this company—it was and is my long-term future, not some woman. Not a family. Thrusting that upon me is about as unfair as it gets, but leave it to the Warrens to do whatever the fuck they want without regard for what their children or grandchildren really want. Either they don't see it, or they don't care. More likely, the latter.

But Blaire saw all of it during the last year she's been here. She saw who and what all these women were—nothing to me.

There isn't anyone here at Warren Enterprises World-wide more qualified to be my executive assistant. And apparently, to help me get my personal life situated, too.

What other options do I have at this point with a ticking clock and five fucking weeks to find someone to marry me? Damn my family.

I sigh and wave a hand at her. "Go ahead, Miss Hall."

Time to hear the master plan.

With my fingers steepled under my chin, I watch Blaire squirm under the pressure of my intense focus.

Those moss-green eyes flick up to mine. "You may not like it, but just hear me out." She shuffles her notepad around on her lap and clears her throat. "You don't want to marry any of your former, ah, um acquaintances."

The nervous tone to her voice has me moving my hand to my lips to stifle a chuckle. I'm sure it isn't easy to speak with your boss so frankly about such a personal topic.

"Well, like I said, they are your ex-girlfriends for a reason. Right?"

I nod my agreement while she appears to search her lap for some confidence. For a woman who doesn't seem to care what anyone thinks of what she wears, she sure seems to lack confidence when she's sitting here across from me. Maybe I've been too harsh on her or haven't shown my appreciation enough, so she thinks I don't want to hear her ideas or suggestions. That isn't true, though, and I hope she does know that.

She takes a shaky breath before meeting my eyes again. "We treat your quest, if you will, as an applicant we would hire to work for the company."

Well, shit.

Before I can react, she continues, "We run an ad for a wife, in the paper, possibly set up a web site. We can have a questionnaire or application for the women to fill out that can help us narrow down the field of appropriate candidates."

Damn, that's not a bad idea.

The Warrens expect a certain type of woman for a family bride. It's one of the reasons they were so adamantly against Artie and Penelope being together when they were younger. If we had an application and made sure to include all the things to fulfill the "Warren bride" checklist, the chances of having any objections from the family would be almost nil. And, I damn sure don't want to be saddled with the likes of Mirabella Owens for the rest of my life. An interview process would help weed out those types of women—ones who will cause nothing but scandal and pain.

But how would this work? And most importantly, what would Father and Grandfather think if they found out?

I push myself up higher in my chair and shuffle some papers on my desk. This entire situation is fucked up...and totally unexpected. I should never have even had this chance. Rightfully, the company was to go to Artie because he was the firstborn, but since he's out of the picture, it opened up the door for me to take what I always wanted. I can't let it go. I can't let the entire family down. If that means pissing off Grandfather and Father—and undoubtedly Mother and Grandmother, as well—by holding future wife auditions, so be it. They're messing with my life, so I have every right to try to make the rest of it bearable by finding a woman I can actually tolerate for longer than a few hours in my bed.

They'd probably shit themselves if they could see me now. This is about the most unprofessional conversation I've ever had with an employee, and it certainly isn't in her work description. Yet, it's given me a glimmer of hope. I can't even believe she came up with this. It's impressive. Now, we just need a game plan because we don't have much time before I have to walk down the aisle.

I clear my throat and hold out my hands, palms up, totally at Blaire's mercy to figure out this mess that is my life. "How do we proceed?"

CHAPTER 3

BLAIRE

Wanted: *one bride for marriage to billionaire heir at New Year's Eve wedding. Submit resume and photo to INEEDAWIFE@wannamarryabillionaire.com*
Qualified candidates must:

- *Be Ivy League educated*
- *Come from a family free of any major scandal*
- *Reside in the greater New York City area and or be willing to relocate immediately*
- *Be amenable to starting a family immediately*
- *Be prepared to attend any and all events as requested and required*

Any candidates not meeting these requirements will not be considered. Please attach a photo, resume, a list of any and all family and relatives including dates of birth, as well as a 500-word essay describing why you think you would be a good match.

I stare down at my notebook at the draft of the "job listing" Archimedes and I just wrote up and cringe.

This is so wrong.

The words on the page make my heart hurt. This isn't any way to find someone to spend your life with. This was a terrible idea. Guilt at having been the one who suggested it in the first place creeps in. I'm the one who told him to treat this with detachment. To look at it like a business deal that he can negotiate and close. It's all so wrong.

I chance a glance in Archie's direction. He's barely moved in his chair over the last hour. Leaned back, his hands steepled under his chin, a furrowed brow, eyes focused somewhere out the window. It seems to be his new normal look, at least since this trust announcement.

It's not like him to appear so stressed...or so unhappy. Archie may be a lot of things, including demanding, but he's generally pretty positive and upbeat. All of this is starting to get to him, and I can't really say I blame him. If I had to rush into a marriage with someone I didn't love just to appease my overbearing family, I'd be miserable and stressed, too.

I tap my pen against my notepad.

Should I say anything?

He was receptive to my earlier comments about Mirabella and the other exes, but there may be a line I cross that I can't come back from, one that would cost me this job.

I chew on my lip and fiddle with my pen, considering my options. Ignore the nagging voice in the back of my head or let it speak and face the consequences? The ache in my chest seems to be making the decision for me.

I have to say something.

"Um, Mister Warren?"

He jerks in his seat, and his head turns until his eyes meet mine. "I'm sorry. Did you say something?"

"Well," I shift in my chair and clear my throat, "I'm just

wondering if you're sure this is all you want me to put in the ad?"

I've read it back to him twice, and both times, he told me it was "sufficient." But I have a difficult time believing that given the way he's acting. And based on human nature.

Humans need more than mere compatibility. Matches that last forever aren't made based on a checklist like this.

Where's the passion? Where's the connection? Where's the love?

"Yes," he nods slowly, "that should check off the boxes of everything I need."

Everything he needs? He can't be serious.

I look over the list again and see all the bullet points that *should* be there but aren't. "But, sir—"

"Jesus, stop calling me *sir*." He scrubs a hand over his face. "Archie, please."

"Mister Warren, I'm not sure I'm comfortable calling you by your first name."

He chuckles and holds up his hands. "You're helping me pick a wife. I think that puts us on a first-name basis."

A smile pulls at my lips. "I guess you're right."

"And I hope you don't mind if I call you Blaire."

"No, sir...I mean Archie. Not at all."

He flashes me a genuine smile, possibly the first real one I've seen from him in days. "I really appreciate your help with this, you know. I understand it's not exactly in your job description."

I chuckle and shake my head. "No, it's not, and neither is saying things that should probably get me fired."

He raises a dark eyebrow at me. "What do you need to say that you think is going to get you fired?"

"Well..." I hold up the list and turn it to face him, "it seems to me you're missing several things here that are incredibly important."

"Really?" His brow furrows again. "Hand it to me." He

reaches across the desk and takes the notebook. His tired eyes scan the words, and he taps his finger against his lips. "Nope. I think that's it."

He can't possibly be this clueless. Can he?

"No, Mister Warr—uh, Archie, I don't think it is. What about chemistry? Connection? What about love?"

He freezes, and his eyes drift up to meet mine. "That sounds like fairy-tale talk, Blaire."

"No." My chest tightens. "It's not a fairy tale. It's what most people experience with the person they're going to spend the rest of their life with. How can you honestly think that you're going to be happy with someone, have children with them, and live with them for the rest of your life if you don't have those things first?"

Archie tosses the notebook across the desk, and it slides off my side and thumps to the travertine tile floor. He pushes up from his chair, shoves his hands into his pockets, and stalks over to the massive windows that overlook the busy street below.

He drops his forehead against the glass and stares out, suddenly not looking like the all-powerful Archimedes Warren anymore. This isn't the strong, confident billionaire heir I know. He looks...lost. "That may be true for other people, Blaire. People who weren't born into the Warren family. But I don't have the luxury of marrying someone I love."

ARCHIMEDES

"Luxury?"

The surprise in her question makes me cringe, and my skin heats even more despite having my forehead pressed against the cool glass. I thought moving over here, getting away from that damn list, might release some of the tension building in me, the feeling that my skin is too tight, but it hasn't worked. And I don't know how to explain any of this to Blaire without revealing all the Warren family's deepest, darkest secrets—the things we've worked so hard to bury deep below the perfect façade.

I drag my head back from the window and glance over my shoulder at her. Sitting there in her Christmas apparel, with the flashing light bulbs around her neck, I can see how she wouldn't understand my situation. People who weren't brought up in a family like the Warrens can't even begin to complete or grasp the lengths we'll go to in order to reach the top.

If she knew what Grandfather and Father—hell, even Mother and Grandmother—have done over the years to get us where we are, she'd either run from this job screaming or be so terrified, she'd never leave for fear of ending up on some blacklist of targets.

You're either with the Warrens or against them. And being one of them means you don't have a choice but to knock down people who stand in your way and face the consequences. It also means accepting that some things will never be part of your life. Love is for poor fools, not rich people who want to keep climbing.

I don't think I've ever seen any genuine affection between any of the married couples in the family—except Artemis and Penelope, but it took separating himself from the Warrens to get it.

No, she can't possibly get it.

"Love is a luxury in this family, Blaire. You may not understand that, and it may seem completely foreign to you, to someone who undoubtedly believes in things like Christmas miracles."

She bites her lip, probably because I'm right. But all it does is draw attention to how beautiful she is, how perfectly bow-shaped that lip is. And so pink. Something I definitely shouldn't be noticing right now while we're talking about finding me a wife. Something I shouldn't have ever noticed since she's my employee.

I turn back to the window and lean one shoulder against it, watching the traffic inch by below through the snow and slush. "The truth is, the Warrens marry for money and prestige...and nothing else."

A silence lingers between us as she considers the weight of my statement before her soft question floats over to me. "You don't think your grandparents love each other...or your parents?"

She's met all of them over her time here when they stopped in for various reasons and at the family Christmas party. But she's never seen them outside the settings where they are one hundred percent in character and obsessively concerned about how they look to the world...how we *all* look to the world. She's only seen the public Warrens, and the ones we become in private are very different.

"Things aren't always what they appear, Blaire. And one thing you'll learn if you're in this business long enough is that if you believe otherwise, you're going to get burned."

"Like you did with Mirabella?"

I chuckle and glance over my shoulder at her. "Yeah. Something like that. You were right in your suggestion that we treat this like we're hiring an employee. I need to keep feelings out of this." I rub the back of my neck to work away some of the tightness there. "It's a business deal. Whoever marries me will get all the power and prestige that comes with my name. And I'm sure my father and grandfather will set up a very generous allowance to keep my wife happy."

"Money doesn't buy happiness."

She's so naïve. The way she says it like it's the most obvious truth in the world. Like it's something I should know and understand.

It hurts me to have to say this to her. "The only people who say that are people who don't have money."

She winces and glances down at herself. Undoubtedly, it was harsh, but the words are true, nonetheless. Blaire and I are from two different worlds, and she couldn't possibly comprehend the stresses and realities of mine. Sometimes, I wish I would have been born into a different life. One where I wasn't constantly living under a microscope and the weight of expectation.

I turn back to face her and cross my arms over my chest. A huge part of me wants to apologize for what I just said, but she needed to hear the harsh truth if she's going to be involved in this process. "Look, Blaire, if you're not comfortable helping me with this because of your feelings on the issue, I understand. I'm not going to ask you to do anything you're not comfortable with, especially because this is not part of your job description. I can find someone else to help me. My sister, Athena. I'm sure Mother and Grandmother have plenty to say on the topic, as well."

"No." Blaire practically leaps from her seat and meets me at the window. "I want to help you."

It seems like she wants to say something more, but she bites it back and holds up the notepad I tossed back to her. "I have the ad here. I will type it up and get it sent out to all the major newspapers..." she hesitates briefly, "if you're one hundred percent sure this is the way you want to do it."

I turn away again to watch all the people skittering back and forth in the falling snow, totally unaware of how lucky they are to have the ability to live their lives the way they see fit. "I don't have a choice, Blaire. Do it."

CHAPTER 4

ARCHIMEDES

The glass door to my office swings open. I don't even bother to look up. Blaire will tell me what she needs or drop off whatever it is she brought.

"What's up your butt today?"

Athena?

I look up from the contracts I've been poring over and narrow my eyes on her. "Nothing. And what are you doing here, anyway?"

She holds up a large paper bag. "You do. I can tell by the scowl on your face. And...here I brought you lunch and thought you might actually be good company."

I snort and shake my head. "Now, what in the world would make you think something stupid as that."

"Ha ha." Athena sets the bag in front of me and drops into the chair facing me. "Will you move all this crap off your desk so we can eat?"

I glance down at the paper spread out across the glossy wooden surface and sigh. "I guess I could use some food."

The break is definitely welcome, too. I'll probably be stuck here late tonight, finalizing this deal, but it's too big to leave in anyone else's hands. Acquiring this company for Warren Enterprises could make us billions. So eating is a good thing.

I stack the pages and spread my hands over the clean surface of the desk. "All clear."

Athena unpacks the bag and places a black plastic take-out container in front of herself and me. "I got you a club sandwich and kettle chips."

"At least you remember what I like."

She grins and drags her chair up closer to the desk so she can sit to eat, then throws a thumb over her shoulder toward Blaire's desk. "What's up with Blaire?"

I follow her line of vision but don't see anything unusual —Blaire on the phone, her red hair tumbling from the clip she tries to contain it in. "I don't know what you mean."

The scent of my sandwich wafts up to my nose, and I take a bite and revel in the flavors dancing against my tongue.

Christ, I didn't realize how hungry I was.

Spending the morning designing the perfect wife will really take it out of you, apparently. But Blaire seems fine, so I don't know what Athena is talking about.

Athena shrugs. "She was just kind of acting weird when I came in."

I raise an eyebrow at her. "Weird how?"

She lifts one shoulder. "I don't know. She was flipping through a huge stack of papers, and it sounded like her printer was running nonstop. She didn't even get up to escort me in here, which she *always* does. She waved a hand to usher me back and grabbed the phone without a word. She just seemed...preoccupied. What's going on?"

"Oh." I swallow and nod. "She's probably just printing out applications."

Athena's brow furrows, and she takes a bite of her pickle. "Applications for what?"

"My wife."

She chokes on her food, and her eyes widen. Something resembling a mix of a cough and gasp slips from her lips, and she pounds on her chest until she can finally swallow. "Your *wife*? Please tell me I heard that wrong."

I shrug as nonchalantly as possible when discussing my future matrimony and take another bite. Athena watches me chew with raised eyebrows and judgment in her matching blue gaze.

Sometimes, it's unnerving how much she can see at such a young age.

I swallow and shift around the pile of chips to avoid her assessment. "She made a very good suggestion that perhaps calling all my exes wasn't the best way to locate the person to spend the rest of my life with. So," I shrug and pop a chip into my mouth, "I created an application."

Athena shakes her head and takes a deep breath. "God, you two are idiots."

"Who? Blaire and me?"

She shakes her head again. "No, you and Artemis."

"Gee, thanks." I shove the sandwich into my mouth to keep myself from saying something else to her that I might regret later.

"But it's true. He gave up on the love of his life and let her walk away when he should've chased after her all those years ago. Because of that, he missed out on a huge chunk of his son's life. Then he gave up the company to get the girl back. And now, here you are, wanting the company, and you're willing to spend your life with someone you might hate just to get it." She circles her hand. "Are you following me here?"

When she puts it that way...I can kind of see what she means.

I lean back in my chair and throw up my hands. "What

the hell am I supposed to do? I have five weeks to get married, or I lose all this."

She looks around and shrugs. "Maybe all this," she waves her hand, "isn't all it's cracked up to be."

I roll my eyes at her and shake my head. "I know *you* have zero interest in working for Warren Enterprises. But just because you and Artie don't want it doesn't mean I shouldn't. You have your dream, so let me have mine."

"And your dream is marrying someone you haven't met yet five weeks prior to the wedding?"

I sigh and take a bite of my sandwich because I don't have an answer to that. At least not one that will appease her.

Of course, I don't *want* to marry someone I barely know. Everyone wants love in their life at some point, I just haven't had the time to look for it, nor have I really been in the market. I thought I had all the time in the world. Now, with a ticking clock, I need to accept the reality of the situation, whether I like it or not.

Athena raises her eyebrow at me again. "What? No answer to that?"

"Shut up and eat your lunch."

A very unladylike snort shoots out with her laugh, and she shakes her head. "Yeah, yeah, okay. What do I know? I'm just the only sane one in the family."

I point a finger at her. "That's debatable."

She grins at me, picking at her bread. Hopefully, she'll let me finish this lunch in peace. God knows I could use it after this day.

"You know who's cute?"

So much for letting me eat in peace.

"Who?"

She peeks over her shoulder. "Blaire. Actually, she's not just cute. She's pretty hot."

I jab a finger at her. "Don't go there."

She holds up her hands in mock surrender, her jaw dropped open. "I'm just saying is all."

Just saying.

"Just saying things like that is what gets people sued for sexual harassment." Besides, I don't need any reminders of how attractive she is. That's like telling someone the sky is blue. I glance out the glass wall of my office at the woman who's going to help me pick my wife. "Even if—for the sake of argument only—I did think Blaire were attractive, it's not like I can date her."

"Why the hell not?" Athena's question comes out more of a mumble around a mouthful of food, but I still manage to decipher it.

"Number one—because she's my employee."

She rolls her eyes.

"And number two—I'm getting married in five weeks."

Athena swallows. "You don't have to get married."

"You don't have to butt into other people's business, yet you can't seem to help yourself."

She shrugs. "You could always just marry *her*."

I bark out a laugh and shake my head. "That's the stupidest thing I've ever heard."

There are so many things wrong with that statement that I don't even think I could count them all if I tried.

Athena leans back in her chair with her arms crossed over her chest. "Is it?"

"Of course, it is." I rest my elbows on the desk and lean forward so I can lower my voice and ensure Blaire won't hear us. "First, and foremost, Blaire would have no interest in that, in me, and second, even if she did, I would never put an employee in that position."

"What position?"

I scoff. "You don't think your boss asking you to marry him poses a problem?"

Athena's nose scrunches up as she thinks, then her eyes brighten. "You could always fire her so you're not her boss anymore."

"Jesus," I chuckle and scrub my hands over my face, "that's even worse. Then I ask and she says no and nails me for both sexual harassment *and* wrongful termination."

Athena points at me. "I see your point, but I feel like there's a way to make it work."

I shake my head. "Drop it."

"Or what?"

"Or I tell Mom and Dad what your real major is."

Managing to hide what she's been up to on the other side of the country has been an impressive feat for Athena. Frankly, I'm proud she's standing up to them and their expectations and making her own plan, but the moment they find out, they'll stop paying her tuition and for her condo, and she'll end up out on her ass with nothing. Artemis and I would help her, of course, but she's still young enough to crave the love of the people who are so unwilling to give it freely. It would kill her to get cut off.

She gasps, and her jaw drops. "You wouldn't."

I grin at her across the desk. "Wouldn't I?"

Deep down, we both know I would never do that and am only joking, but it's still fun to mess with her.

"You play dirty, Archimedes Warren."

She says it like it's an insult.

"That's why I always win."

BLAIRE

"Hey, Blaire!"

I jerk around in time to see Athena slide onto the edge of

my desk, balancing herself precariously next to my snow globes. I didn't even hear her approach over the sound of the never-ending printer.

The constant noise in the background all morning has started to turn my brain into mush. Or maybe that's just from looking at these applications and Archie's options for a wife.

She grins at me and swishes her dangling legs back and forth. "Sorry, I didn't mean to scare you."

"It's okay." I twist my necklace around and glance at Archie's office. With his phone pressed to his ear and head buried in a stack of contracts, he seems oblivious to the fact that Athena didn't leave and is instead interrupting my work.

"We really didn't get a chance to chat when I came in." She smiles at me, and something twinkles in her blue eyes that I never see in her brother's—a lightness, almost playfulness. I might even call it mischief if I didn't know better. Given that she's only a few years younger than me, it doesn't surprise me that she's the most laid back and unencumbered of the Warren children. She has to be to survive them and not get eaten alive.

Athena nods toward the printer. "Are those the applications?"

I narrow my eyes on her. "Archie told you?"

She stills for a second, then grins. "He lets you call him Archie?"

I freeze.

Shit. Maybe I shouldn't have said that...

Calling your boss by his nickname is very informal, not exactly something they embrace here at Warren Enterprises. In fact, the formalities are stuck to with such strength and purpose, I think most employees would probably shit themselves if they heard me call him that. It suggests a familiarity between us, one that would certainly be fodder for all sorts of gossip. But this is Athena I'm talking to, and the cat is already out of the bag, so it's best just to plow ahead and act like it isn't a big deal. "Yeah, he asked me to."

She swings her legs back and forth and gives me a look that says she's reading an awful lot into that fact. "Interesting. And yes, he told me about your little plan to find him a wife. I have to say, it's an out-of-the-box idea."

I shake my head and chuckle. "It's a lot better than his plan."

"Oh, the calling the exes thing?" She waves her hand at me. "I know. He would've ended up with Mirabella, and I probably would've ended up killing the bitch."

I gape at her. Not that I don't agree with the sentiment, but for someone like Athena Warren to threaten to kill someone—at least outside of the family where I'm sure threats like that get tossed around daily—is unusual.

She feigns innocence. "Oh, I'm sorry. Was that too forward of me?" A deep chuckle floats from her lips. "After what she did to my brother, if that bitch were stupid enough ever to show her face here again, I would definitely have something to say about it. She's lucky I haven't run into her out in California."

"When do you go back?"

"End of the week. We have finals the second week of December."

"Then, are you coming home for break?"

She shakes her head. "No. I have an internship set up."

"How do your Mom and Dad feel about that?"

Her light laugh tinkles through the air. "I don't care. But apparently, my brother still does, or he wouldn't be jumping through these stupid hoops."

I shrug and absently flip through the first couple pages of the top application. "I still can't believe how fast these are coming in. Or how many."

Athena snorts. "It doesn't surprise me. Nothing stays secret in this building. I bet they knew even before you put out the ad, and once you did, it spread like wildfire."

I nod. "I figured most people had already heard about changes in the trust."

"Can I have a look at those?" She points toward the applications.

I hesitate. "Did Archie ask you to look through them?"

She narrows her eyes on me. "No, but I'm his sister. I should have a chance to look at the candidates applying to be my new sister-in-law."

I guess she does have a point there.

If anyone knows what Archie needs in a bride, it would be Athena. I hand her a stack and grab a second one off the printer. "God, there are so many!"

She snorts. "It's practically a tidal wave of applications."

"Does that make it a bridal wave?"

Her laughter reverberates off the tile floors and hard furniture, and she slaps her hand over her mouth and glances toward Archie's office, but he's on the phone and doesn't seem to have noticed. "That's a good one." She turns her attention to the application on top of the stack and barks out a laugh. "Wilhelmina Everett? You can shred this one now."

"Why? What's wrong with her?"

She shakes her head. "What *isn't* wrong with her is the better question. Trust me; you don't want her anywhere near Archie." She flips through the stack and freezes. "But this one...this one is interesting."

I take it from her. "Regina Boseman? I don't think I know her."

A sly grin spreads across Athena's lips. "Let's just say I think she and Archie have a lot in common."

The tiniest twinge of what can only be jealousy hits my chest. "Really? Like?"

"Their love of money and power. Put this on the top of the stack."

Money and power.

Two things I couldn't care less about.

Yes, I need money to live, but it doesn't define me or make me happy. It may take me years to save up for my dream trip, while people like Regina Boseman and the Warrens can fly off anywhere they want at the drop of a hat without a second thought. But working for something makes it mean more. I'd rather know I earned it than have it handed to me on a silver platter.

Not that Archie doesn't work. He does. *Hard.*

When I came to work for him, Artie had only recently left and things were still very unstable. With their father in the Senate and spending a lot of time in Washington and their Grandfather essentially retired, it was left to Archie to step up and take the reins of this company even at quite a young age. I respect that he works hard for what he wants, even though I question the means he's willing to go to in order to keep it—like this sham of a marriage.

Athena spends another few minutes looking for candidates and hands me a stack. "Put these on top." Then, she hands me another stack. "Shred these."

"Why?"

She winks at me. "Because sister always knows best." With that, she slips away toward the elevator with a glance over her shoulder. "Have a wonderful Christmas if I don't see you before I leave."

I look at this first couple of applications on the top of the stack. I don't recognize any of the names, but, at initial glance, the women appear picture-perfect and they check off all the boxes.

We'll give it another day or two for applications before we weed through them. Then, next week, it's going to get down to the real nitty-gritty. He needs to actually start meeting some of these girls fast if he has any chance of determining who might make the best wife *and* manage to plan a wedding in a month.

Something tells me this will be one hella busy Christmas season, and I'm going to need the eggnog spiked to make it through.

CHAPTER 5

BLAIRE

I tap the stack of applications on my desk one last time to straighten them, then make my way toward Archie's office, a knot in my stomach.

Why am I so nervous to go through these with him?

For the past two days, I've been sifting through the "keepers" Athena gave me to keep on top, as well as some new ones that have come in that I did an initial screening on, and I've been trying to spot any red flags. A few were obvious, and frankly, I'm surprised Athena missed the issues when she looked at some of them. But after pulling those and promptly shredding them, along with most of the new applications, I'm confident what is in my hand is the best of the best of the applicants.

No one screamed, "I'm Archie's soulmate," but there are some promising candidates. Definitely people who check the boxes he assured me were most important.

So, this shouldn't make me nervous, yet I can't stop the churning in my stomach or the shaking of my hand. Maybe it's because I actually care about Archie and don't want him to spend the rest of his life miserable, or maybe it's because if he ends up miserable, he'll be unmanageable in the office. Either way, I hate feeling like this—like someone's life is literally in my hands.

I take a deep, fortifying breath and knock lightly before pushing open the door. "Archie? Do you have a moment to sort through the applicants?"

He pushes back into his chair, rubbing at his eyes and releases a heavy sigh. The man looks utterly exhausted, and he should be. This deal he's working on is huge, plus this trust business. The toll of the new demands being placed on him are starting to show. "Yes. Please come in, Blaire."

With each step I take on my way to the chair in front of him, the weight of what lies in my hand grows until it feels like a rock that might pull me over. I slowly lower myself into my seat and glance down at the stack. One of the recommendations Athena pulled sits on top.

So, this is it.

One of these women will have her life changed entirely in a matter of a few weeks. Archie will have his wife and his future as the head of this company secured. So much wealth tied up in the dollars' worth of paper sitting in my lap.

Finding a spouse this way is pure insanity, at best. And I'm the one who suggested it.

What was I thinking?

Archie leans forward and rests his elbows on the desk, his eyebrows raised. "So, how'd we end up doing?"

His silvery-blue eyes stare at me with just a hint of hope.

I can't bear to let him down, so I plaster on what I hope is a believable smile. "There are some real winners here." I lift the stack and shake it like the saddest trophy in the world. "I'm positive you'll find the perfect woman here."

The words burn like acid coming from my lips because I

don't believe them. Not for a moment. This just isn't the way to determine the rest of your life.

"Well," he shrugs nonchalantly, but the tension and concern in his body show with the simple movement, "here goes nothing."

He reaches out for the stack and places it in front of him on the desk. For a moment, he studies it, his hands palm-down on either side. He squints and leans in one direction, then the other.

What is he doing?

I shift in my seat and wring my hands in my lap. "Is there a problem, Archie?"

With his focus still on the pile, he points. "This is it? This is all?"

"Yes, sir."

His head snaps up, and his eyes lock on to mine.

Oh, crap.

"Sorry, I meant yes, Archie. Habit." I offer an apologetic smile and shrug. After a year of calling him *sir*, just stopping, especially when I'm flustered and uncomfortable, is more difficult than he can imagine.

He focuses his attention back to the stack. He doesn't need to know Athena cut out over half of the applicants for whatever reason she may have had.

Who am I to question her?

She knows her brother better than I do, and he certainly shouldn't waste countless hours considering women who will never work for his needs.

His needs.

It makes it sound so cold. But that's the point, after all. To make a business decision.

Archie shakes his head. "Huh. Not to sound full of myself, Blaire, but I just thought there'd be more applicants than this."

I hide my smile behind my hand and shift to sit up a bit straighter. No need to fuel his ego by confirming anything.

"Regina Boseman? Regina Boseman. Why does this name ring a bell?"

He grabs the picture and examines it, his interest evident.

And why wouldn't he be interested? She's striking in the black and white photo wearing a gorgeous vintage lace dress and sprawled out on a leather chaise, a book in one hand, a glass of what I presume is fancy wine in the other.

He scans her application, undoubtedly taking note of all the right boxes being ticked.

Ivy league. Wealthy. Beautiful. His gaze flicks up to me momentarily. "What do you think about her?"

Desperate. Vapid.

What type of woman applies for a husband?

The desperate type, I suppose. But I can't say that out loud. Not to Archie. Because it's as much of a statement about him as it is about her.

Instead, I just nod and smile. "She checks all the boxes."

"She does." He nods slowly. "She definitely fits the bill." After one last look at her photo, he places her application face-down onto the desk to his left.

That must be his *keep* pile.

He pulls the second application from the stack, unclips her picture, and looks it over briefly before examining her file. "Jessica Sims. It says she works for the city in public administration. Did you take a look at this one?"

Of course, I did. I read them all, and I had a feeling he'd like this one. True *Warren material* if I've ever seen it. "I did. She seems well-suited."

Not exactly a glowing recommendation for a prospective romantic partner, but there's not really much else I can say. On paper, she seems like a good match for him. Perfect, actually.

He looks at her picture again before laying her resume face down on the keep pile.

Two for two.

I would have thought he would be a little more selective in choosing potential brides, but maybe Athena's choices are just that spot-on.

He picks up the next candidate's information; a small frown mars his brow. "Julie Kline, hard pass." He lays her application face down to his right. "We dated in prep school. She was demanding for an eighth-grader. I can't imagine that has changed with time."

My laugh escapes before I can stop it. "You can't be serious? A demanding eighth-grader?"

He chuckles a moment, his eyes flashing with humor. "Oh, but I am. She would call me the night before school and demand we wear matching outfits. There's only so much of that a man can take."

We devolve into a fit of shared laughter, and honestly, it helps to ease a bit of the tension in the room. Picking one's future wife is a serious exercise, but the entire situation is so insane, it's good to have something to laugh about.

Matching outfits. I bet Archie was adorable as a child. His dark hair and striking eyes likely had all the girls lining up. Not much has changed, really. Given the number of applications I shredded, he had more than half the damn city lining up to say, "I do."

But only one woman is going to get that lucky. I hope she knows what she has.

ARCHIMEDES

Blaire wasn't kidding when she said she was hungry an hour ago. Sitting across my desk from me, wearing today's God-awful outfit, shoveling noodles into her mouth at record speed, she looks like a woman who hasn't eaten in days rather than merely hours. Though, it is almost seven, far later than I would normally keep her at work, so I guess I can't really blame her for being starved.

I hide my smile behind my napkin and watch her eat.

God, she's adorable.

The black dress covered in metallic-gold deer paired with knee-high boots is kind of oddly sexy on her, and one thing I can really appreciate is a woman who isn't afraid to *eat*. Nothing is more annoying than going on a date with a woman to a nice restaurant for a fantastic meal only to have her order a side salad because she's afraid to let a man watch her enjoy food or is too self-conscious about consuming a few extra calories.

Those extra calories are what give women curves—beautiful, luscious curves that give you something to hold on to and revel in.

She catches me staring and pauses mid-bite. "What? Do I have sauce on my face or something?"

Shit. I shouldn't be checking out my secretary.

And if I don't stop, I may end up with an uncomfortable situation in my pants in a few minutes.

I blame it on this damn Warren bride search. Ever since I read the words on the trust documents on Thanksgiving, everywhere I look, I end up checking out women with one thing on my mind—whether or not she's good marriage material. Not whether I'm attracted to them. Not whether it's someone I would *want* to go out on a date with or even hook up with for a one-night stand.

Marriage material!

What a fucking travesty. Getting cut down in my prime.

It's left me in this weird headspace that I'll blame for my ogling of Blaire.

"Nothing." I divert her attention by pulling the stack of applications back toward me and pick up the next one on top. "Are you kidding me? Did you put this in here as a joke?"

Her eyes bounce over toward me. "I don't think so. What is it?"

I look down again to be sure I'm reading this correctly. "Doctor Cosette Archambeau; specializing in Kamasutra instruction."

Blaire snorts out an incredulous laugh. "Stop it. You're kidding me."

She stands and rounds my desk to lean over my shoulder and examine the paper. The smell of the spicy noodles she just inhaled hits my nose. Her shoulder brushes against mine. A little zing of electricity shoots through my arm and into my hand.

Christ, she's close.

Too close.

I shake my head to clear the thoughts forming there and motion toward the application. "Oh, I am so not kidding. Definitely heading to the keep pile."

I start to lay it on the *keep stack*, but Blaire yanks it away from my hand.

"Hey!" I jerk my head toward her. "What are you doing?"

"Definitely not." She shakes her head, a strange look on her face—a mix of amusement and maybe annoyance. "If anyone is a firm no, it's the good doctor." She places the paper onto the growing stack of discarded applicants.

"Can we at least put her in the *maybe* pile?"

Blaire scowls. "Can you honestly say your family would approve of her job?"

That's a definite no.

No fun in my marriage bed for me, that is.

"Okay, next." I reach for the next candidate, and instantly, the smile in her picture draws me in. The sun hits her face in just the right way, where she sits on a bench in the park.

She's actually quite lovely. Dark-blond hair, blue eyes, and a mesmerizing smile. It's all very girl-next-door, and she exudes a soft, welcome warmth.

I tilt the photo toward Blaire, who still stands behind me —way too closely. "What do you think about her? Daniella Storm."

"Well, I like that." She uses her chopstick to point at her job, a pharmaceutical rep. "She must be good with people if she does that, right? Plus, she looks happy and wholesome. Definitely a keeper."

I lay it on top of the keep pile, which at this point, is a lot smaller than I thought it would be. For some reason, I imagined a ton of candidates who would be perfect, but there are only three applications there after all these hours of weeding through them. Only three I looked at and actually thought *yeah, she could be my wife.*

It's depressing, really. Such a fucked-up way to find a spouse.

Blaire returns to her seat and continues to eat while I look through the last few applications in the stack, shifting them all over to the *absolutely not* pile. Then I grab the three keepers and spread them out in front of me to examine again.

I've already wasted a week setting up this entire screening process, which only leaves me a month to make one of these three women my bride. Four short weeks to meet someone, get to know them, propose, hope they accept, plan a wedding, and get hitched.

Which means...I need to get a move-on.

"Blaire, I'll need you to set up a lunch date with these ladies, please. Just pick a spot with a bit of privacy that's close enough for us to walk to and arrange a time that works with my schedule. Do one a day, starting on Monday."

She sets down her takeout container, stabs the chopsticks into it, and sighs. "So, you're really going to do this?"

Her question echoes the one that's been floating around my head all week.

Am I really going to do this? Am I really going through with this insanity?

I run my hand over my jaw and sigh. "It's insane, right?"

She nods slowly. "A little bit."

"So is forcing my assistant to spend a week writing an ad and weeding through applications...for my *wife.*"

A grin pulls at her lips. "You didn't force me to do anything, Archie. I'm glad I could help. Really. It's okay."

"No," I shake my head. "It's not. I really appreciate all you've done. And I am going through with this, which means I'm going to need even more assistance. I have no idea how to plan a wedding, and I don't think we can wait until I have a decision on who the bride will be to start planning."

"You're right. Venues will already be booked, especially for a New Year's Eve wedding. Then there's the cake, decorations, flowers—"

I hold up a hand to stop her. "Your list alone is giving me anxiety. I hate to ask, but can you take care of all of that? Make sure everything is covered? I'm sure Mom and Grandmother would leap at the chance to do it, but I can't bear the thought of them having their hands in my life any more than they do."

Blaire considers my request for a moment, then gives me a smile that doesn't quite touch her eyes. "Of course, I'll help. Don't worry. I know just what to do."

CHAPTER 6

The elevator dings, announcing the arrival of Daniella Storm, contestant number one in *Who Wants to Marry a Billionaire?*

I hold my breath as the doors slide open. She was one of Athena's picks, and also one of the applicants Archie and I seemed to agree on, so I hope that means good things for the date. Archie is way too stressed out right now and needs some sort of resolution so he can have forward movement on this before he drops from a coronary.

It's why we scheduled the dates with the top three applicants this week. If none of them pan out, he'll move on to our second-tier group, the people who have promise but who don't exactly jump out at him as the perfect candidate.

But we don't have much time left, and with the big acquisition scheduled to become final soon, the last thing Archie needs is this deadline for marriage hanging over his head like a guillotine threatening to fall.

It's why I agreed to plan the wedding for him even with

no bride. I've had the perfect ceremony in my head since I was a child and created a book with photos for inspiration, so at least I have some idea where to start, though planning it so fast is going to take a *lot* of string-pulling and money being thrown around. Archie directed me to do whatever it took to get it done, carte blanche.

And I'll take that and run with it. Let's just hope one of these women is *the one.*

The elevator doors finally open, but the girl who walks out in the sky-high Louboutins is *not* the same girl in the picture we looked at last week.

This can't be right.

I glance down at her file laid out on my desk in front of me and the photo attached. The girl making her way over to me across the tile has had so much plastic surgery since this photo was taken that she's almost unrecognizable.

Narrower nose. Puffier, plump lips that make her look like she just got stung by a bee and has some sort of allergic reaction that requires immediate attention. Eyebrows so thin they look painted on. And if I'm not mistaken, cheek implants and a chin adjustment of some sort.

Yikes.

Gone is the sweet-looking girl next door with the dish-water-blond hair. This bleached-blond version looks more like Plastic Surgery Barbie—all the things that made her *her* no longer visible.

I swallow thickly and plaster on a fake smile. "Hello."

She flashes me a dazzling white smile. *Too* white. With teeth so perfect, they must be caps. "I'm here to see Archimedes Warren. *We* have a lunch date."

Ugh...

The way she said that like she's bragging to me about having a date with Archie makes me gag. This one isn't going to make the cut. I can tell it immediately and have a feeling

Archie isn't going to be enthralled with the attitude she's already throwing around.

But despite my shock, I maintain my composure and smile at her.

Her blue eyes travel over my desk, across all my Christmas snow globes, and then to my Rudolph sweater, complete with blinking red nose, and she smirks. "Well, you certainly have a unique...*style*. I can't say I've ever met a grown woman so obsessed with childish things like Christmas who also enjoys dressing like a toddler."

I bite back the retort at the tip of my tongue because it's not in my job description to tell off anyone, and even though I think Archie would understand it in this case, I'm too much of a professional to let her get to me.

Instead, I rise from my chair and sweep a hand toward the black leather couch against the side wall of the small waiting area. It's specifically for the executive floor that houses Archie and his father's offices. "Please take a seat, and I'll see if Mister Warren is ready."

She gives me another fake smile and saunters over there, her attention zeroing in on the Picasso and Rembrandt hanging in the reception area.

Probably wondering how much they're worth if she were to sell them...if she even knows what they are, that is.

I grit my teeth and make my way to Archie's office. With his face buried in a stack of papers on his desk, he doesn't even notice my approach, even though he could see me through the glass if he bothered to look up. I knock on the door, and he jerks up his head and raises an eyebrow.

His normally bright-blue eyes, clouded by stress and lack of sleep, meet mine. "She here?"

Depends on who he's expecting.

The girl from the picture most certainly is *not* here.

I step in and let the door close behind me. "Yes."

55

"Why didn't you just buzz me?"

"Well...there's something I should warn you about first."

He groans and leans back in his chair. "Oh, hell. I can't handle any more surprises."

I suppress a grimace and take a seat across from him. "Her picture isn't exactly an accurate depiction of her current appearance. Let's just put it that way."

His brow furrows, and he narrows his eyes on me. "How much different can it be?"

It's impossible to stop the chuckle that rises in my throat, and I shrug. "About ten surgeries worth is my light estimate."

He scowls and shakes his head. "It can't be that bad. My mom has had a couple of nips and tucks here and there, but she looks great."

I open my mouth to say something but bite it back. He waits for me to speak, but I refuse. I don't want to sound like a catty bitch in front of my boss. Even though things have definitely been more casual and comfortable between us lately, I'm constantly worried about crossing a line I won't be able to come back from. One that would get me fired.

His mouth drops open. "Wow, is it really that bad?"

Yes. Absolutely yes.

I give him a look and shrug. "The words *Plastic Surgery Barbie* come to mind."

"Oh, Lord." He pushes to his feet and sucks in a deep breath. "Thanks for the warning. But appearances aren't everything, right?"

"No, they certainly aren't."

But this one lacks a decent personality, too.

It's what I want to say. But I don't. Archie may have wanted my help in weeding through all these candidates, but I doubt he needs my commentary on the girls' personalities or attitudes. He'll experience it himself soon enough.

He grabs his suit coat off the hanger on the wall and

shrugs it on. "How do I look?"

I let my gaze devour him in the perfectly tailored navy suit that makes his eyes even bluer, crisp white shirt with the top two buttons open, and shiny black loafers. "Like you just stepped off the cover of *GQ Magazine*."

His lips pull up into the grin that always sends my heart flip-flopping. "Thanks, Blaire. I don't know what I would do without you."

The compliment makes my heart spasm again.

Knock it off, Blaire. He's your boss. He's talking about your assistance with work.

He starts for the door. "I guess I'll see you after lunch."

I nod and jump up to open the door for him. He squares his shoulders and strolls out to the waiting area with a fake smile on his face. He's going to need to use that a lot during this lunch.

ARCHIMEDES

"And how much would my monthly stipend be?"

I look up from my barely touched chicken caesar salad at the woman sitting across from me. "Excuse me?"

There's no way possible I heard that right.

"Oh. I asked what my monthly stipend would be. You know, spending money. Unless you're just going to give me access to all your accounts." She grins at me like the question isn't the most insulting thing you can ask someone.

Although, it's definitely not the most insulting thing she's asked me over this terrible lunch. This might be the worst forty-five minutes of my life thus far. And that's saying a lot considering all the Warren bullshit I've dealt with for so long.

This woman is so vapid that it's like talking to dead air.

Dead air who wants a big payday. But maybe that's my fault. Maybe I was naïve to think any woman responding to the ad would treat this like anything other than a business deal.

That was the whole point, wasn't it?

Blaire's brilliant idea to treat this with a *hearts off* approach appeared reasonable at the time. Instead of looking for love, look for somebody I can tolerate long enough to get what I want. But this all seemed easier in theory than it appears to be in reality.

I offer Daniella a fake smile, the one I've been using all lunch, and shrug as nonchalantly as I can. "My accounts will stay mine. Just as anything you had prior to the marriage will remain yours."

The plastic-perfect smile she's been wearing since we got here falters, and she frowns, but her face barely moves. "So, I won't have access to any of the Warren money?"

The Warren money...

I grit my teeth and glance around the busy restaurant. Originally, I wanted this place because it's close to the office and easy to get to, but now I regret the fact that so many people I know, including several employees, are sitting around us and may overhear or see something I don't want them to.

"We would be signing a prenup. One that would lay out what you would be receiving while we are married."

"And how long do we need to keep this up?"

This time, I grit my teeth so hard I actually feel something crack in the back. "The way the trust is written, indefinitely. If we got divorced, or if we don't have a child within a year, I would lose my role as CEO and access to any of the family funds."

Her jaw drops. "We need to have kids?"

I nod slowly. "That's a stipulation in the trust."

"You can't be serious."

"Why is it such a crazy idea that you have a child with your husband?"

She scoffs and waves her hand up and down the front of her fake breasts. "Have you *seen* this body? I'm not getting pregnant and ruining all of this. I paid too much for it."

I attempt to open my mouth and find some words, but she's rendered me literally speechless.

Her eyes widen slightly, and she holds up a perfectly manicured finger. "Although, I suppose you could just pay to have me fixed up after. And we can have an *au pair* handle a child twenty-four seven. Just one correct?"

"Yeah, just one." I've only had one date and I'm already on the verge of slitting my wrists. I push my plate back and wave over the waiter. "Can you just put this on my account, please?"

He nods. "Absolutely, Mister Warren. Thank you for joining us. Is there anything else I can do for you today?"

Besides drop this bitch in the East River so no one is ever subjected to her again?

I smile at him, the first genuine one I've had almost all day except for when Blaire was in my office. "I'm good. Thanks."

Even one more minute sitting here will be too many. I push back my chair and rise to my feet.

Daniella gapes. "What are you doing?"

I button my suit coat and brush my hands over it to get out any wrinkles. "What does it look like I'm doing? I'm leaving."

"Why?"

Her question comes out so high-pitched and whiny that she sounds more like a petulant child than an adult woman.

I bite the side of my cheek to keep myself from saying something that would be out of her mouth and into the ears of every socialite in New York in ten minutes. I have to maintain the Warren composure, no matter how badly I want to break it. "It was lovely to meet you, Daniella, but I don't think that this is going to work."

She scoffs and pushes her breasts out, like showing me even more cleavage might make me change my mind. "Why not?"

I shrug slightly.

What can I tell her that won't get a drink thrown in my face or make me look like more of a dick than she's already going to tell people I am?

"I'm just not feeling the spark here."

Her eyes widen like she can't believe I would say that. "I think we get along great."

Was she sitting at the same table as me? Have we not been having the same conversation?

This woman is an absolute nut job.

"I'm sorry it's not going to work, Daniella. I wish you the best of luck in all your future endeavors."

"My future endeavors? But what about—"

I hold up a hand to stop her. "There's no point continuing with this. You're only going to embarrass yourself more."

Her jaw drops open. "You bastard."

Okay, maybe that comment went a little bit too far, but how can she not realize how she comes across? How can she not feel even the least bit bad about how she's acting?

I turn and retreat, leaving her mouth hanging open as she watches me leave the restaurant. The coat check woman hands me my jacket, and I shrug into it as I step out into the snowy New York day. A cab flies by on the street, blaring its horn at pedestrians crossing against the light, and I suck in a deep breath of the familiar smog-filled air.

Only today, it's mixed with the crisp scent of falling snow, and it's almost refreshing, especially after being cooped up in there with that psycho for an hour. If I had known how rough that would be, I never would've gone down this route or picked her as one of my potential candidates.

How could Blaire and I both have been so wrong about her?

Maybe because she looked so sweet and innocent in her photo. Things apparently changed fast for her.

Just like they have for me

This entire process seems like it's not going very well. But at this point, I've wasted too much time, and there's no other choice but to forge ahead.

I set out on the sidewalk toward the office and push my way inside the revolving glass door. Rinaldo, our head of security, waves at me from his post, and I wave back and make my way into the executive elevator. I press my finger to the scanner, and it registers and shoots up to the executive floor. When the doors open and I step out, Blaire's gaze meets mine, and she raises her eyebrows hopefully.

"So, how was it?"

A sigh slips from my lips, and I step up to her desk. "Let me put it this way—I would be better off marrying an actual Barbie doll than that woman."

Blaire barks out a laugh and slaps her hands over her mouth, eyes wide. "Oh, crap. I'm sorry, sir. I shouldn't have laughed like that. It was rude and unprofessional—"

I hold up a hand to stop her and give her a reassuring smile. "Nothing to apologize for, Blaire. She deserves a laugh like that."

"So, can I safely assume she's out of the running?"

I scrub a hand over my face. "She's at the bottom of the barrel."

Blaire offers me a sympathetic smile, then grabs the woman's file off her desk and pushes it through the shredder. The sound of the machine destroying her application and that old photo is the second most beautiful sound I've ever heard...just short of Blaire's laughter over it.

CHAPTER 7

ARCHIMEDES

The bright, cold winter sun shining outside reflects off the ice and snow in Central Park, but I can't look away, despite it almost blinding me. I thought maybe staring at it, taking in the beauty of the winter wonderland Blaire seems so fond of would improve my mood, but I've been standing at this window for more than half an hour, and I still feel like hitting something.

Or someone.

Everything is fucked up with the acquisition, and no matter how many times I've tried a different tactic, I just can't get them to commit to signing the papers. It's frustrating beyond belief and looks like an epic failure as interim and, hopefully, future CEO.

On top of that, dodging Father and Grandfather's calls is becoming increasingly more difficult. The last angry message on my voicemail made it clear how they feel about my little ad in no uncertain terms. *"An uncouth and demeaning display,"* were the exact words, if I remember correctly.

And I have to admit that after that disastrous meeting with Daniella on Monday, I'm having second thoughts about this whole process.

I glance at my watch. 12:02. My second candidate should be arriving any minute now. I'm glad I gave myself the day off yesterday from meeting with any of these women. God knows I sure as hell needed it to recover from Daniella.

But this one looks promising. Regina Boseman. She has the perfect background and a beautiful photo. The name sounded familiar, but I couldn't quite place her. I guess I'll figure out where I might know her from soon.

The sharp knock on my door jerks me from my thoughts, and I wave in Blaire. Her green Christmas tree dress, complete with varied levels and the hoop skirt at the bottom to give it the realistic shape makes me chuckle every time I see it. She glares at me and gives me that *shut the hell up* look that's so damn adorable, but I know she won't say it. Not when I'm her boss.

"Your father called again. *Twice.*"

"I know. Called my cell, too. What did you tell him?"

"That you were in a meeting about the acquisition and that I expected you to be unavailable all day."

I release a sigh and grin at her. "Thank you. At least that bought me a little time."

She tips her head to the side, her red hair spilling over her shoulder. "Aren't you afraid he or your grandfather is just going to show up here if you keep avoiding their calls?"

"Nah." I shake my head and button my suit coat. "Dad is in DC finishing up some stuff before Congress goes on break and my grandfather and grandmother are in Florida until right before Christmas. I'm in the clear, at least for a little while."

Her lips screw down in a frown. "You can only avoid your father for so long, you know."

I sigh and nod. "That's the problem with the Warrens. They always find you and manage to get under your skin."

"Don't I know it."

"What?"

She cringes, and her pale cheeks flush with embarrassment. "Sorry, I didn't realize I said that out loud."

"Am I that bad to work for?"

Her eyes widen, fear flashing in the dark green. "Oh, no, I didn't mean it like that, sir. I—"

I smirk at her and hold out a hand. "I'm just kidding, Blaire. Relax."

She sighs, releasing the tension in her shoulders, and we share a chuckle. I know I'm not the easiest boss in the world and can be demanding, but Blaire handles it with such skill and poise, it barely fazes her.

Even this wedding thing hasn't seemed to make her stumble at all. She's plowing ahead with plans and trying to find the ideal location while I find the perfect wife.

And my watch tells me it's time for my big date. "Is she here yet?"

Blaire fights a grin and nods slowly. "Yes, that was the other reason I came in."

Oh, hell. I know that look.

"What's wrong with this one?"

She smirks and shrugs. "Let's just say she's another outdated-picture situation."

I groan and drop my forehead against the glass. A gust of wind blows snowflakes up against the window. It looks cold, but also, oddly inviting. I wish I were out there enjoying it instead of about to go on what sounds like it might be another disastrous date. "Another plastic surgery addict?"

Her laughter floats across the room to me. "Not quite."

"Then what?" I turn back to her. "Give me a little info here so I don't walk out totally in the dark."

She laughs again, pulls the door open, and steps halfway through. "Oh, seeing your reaction to this one is going to be half the fun."

I drop my jaw open at her as she backs out of my office and lets the door close behind her. Blaire is taking far too much enjoyment in my misery. But I guess she deserves to find a little joy after all the time and energy she's putting into this.

But it's time to meet Regina.

Please, God, let this one be a keeper.

My soul can't handle another minute spent with someone as insipid as Daniella Storm again.

I follow after Blaire, her warm, sweet scent still floating through the air, and I inhale a deep breath. As much as I make fun of and find amusement in all of her Christmas crap, her smelling like sugar cookies isn't unpleasant. It puts a smile on my face as I step out into the waiting area and freeze.

The woman sitting on the leather couch is most *certainly* a different version of the one whose picture we looked at.

A decade or two older, at least.

And the name finally clicks in my head.

She used to babysit for us when we were little. Her parents are friends with Grandmother and Grandfather.

Oh, shit.

BLAIRE

I probably shouldn't have said that to Archie and joked about his misery. But honestly, after the one on Monday, when I saw Regina Boseman walk in here and realized how much older she is than her photo, I couldn't help but completely lose my composure.

And I was right about it being fun to keep the mystery. Watching Archie's reaction was priceless. If I had warned him, I would've completely missed the opportunity to witness the expression on his face. And that would've been a real shame.

Archie plastering on that Warren smile and charm when I can tell he wants to run and hide in his office instead is absolutely the humor I needed today. Even his glower at me as he led the much older woman onto the elevator couldn't stop my fit of laughter.

I might be getting fired for this. But it was worth it.

Definitely worth it.

Now, I'm just waiting for him to return to get all the dirt on the date. I mean, unless I'm totally wrong about Regina and there's a true love connection between them. Maybe Archie is into cougars, but I always thought he was more of a dog person than a cat person.

My cell phone buzzes in my purse, and I reach down to check it. While I typically wouldn't answer personal calls while at work, I need to check and make sure it's nothing important, and with Archie away, it's not like anyone is here to catch me, anyway.

A message from Archie?

He almost never contacts me on my cell phone unless it's an after-hours emergency. And he definitely doesn't text.

Call my phone with some sort of an emergency to get me the hell out of here.

I chuckle and write back to him. *Come on, it can't be that bad.*

The woman is 60! And she used to BABYSIT for us! When I told her we needed to have children to comply with the trust, she started talking about artificial insemi-

nation and all this other shit. I excused myself to the bathroom to try to escape. So, help me!!!

What do I get out of it?

The three little dots that indicate he's replying pop up, and I wait for his witty comeback to my playful text.

You get to keep your job.

I freeze.

He can't be serious. He must be joking. Shit, but what if he's not?

The time for messing with Archie is over. It's time to get back into assistant mode to help him—or I might pay the price later.

Okay, I'll call in two minutes.

He doesn't respond, and I watch the clock tick by slowly.

One minute.

Two.

Time to save the boss from a vicious cougar. I grab the office phone and dial him.

"Archimedes Warren."

"Hello, Mister Warren, I'm calling to let you know we have a *major* emergency at the office. We *desperately* need you to come back."

I can picture his sneer at my emphasis on the words and my playful tone. I might pay for this later, but I can't help myself. The situation is just too funny.

"Thank you for calling, Miss Hall. I'll be right back."

He ends the call, and I drop the phone into the base and lean back in my chair. So far, my great idea for finding Archie a wife is going to shit.

Strike two.

A big one.

I glance at his calendar. Contestant number three is supposed to be here Friday. And if she doesn't pan out, I don't know what he's going to do. He'll be down to three weeks to find someone, and I don't think he wants to delve into the back-up pile.

I just hope he doesn't fire me since it was my idea. Or because I can't stop laughing at his misfortune.

The elevator door slides open with the ding, and Archie storms out, his cheeks pink—but whether from the cold or his anger, I don't know. He glowers at me, slips off his jacket, and tosses it onto my lap.

"Bad date?"

He scowls and slams his palms against my desk. One of my snow globes lurches and teeters on the edge, and I lunge forward to grab it, but not fast enough. It crashes to the tile floor and shatters, sending shards of glass, water, and fake snow across the floor.

"No!"

Archie jumps back and stares down at the carnage. "Shit. I'm sorry, Blaire. I didn't mean to."

I clench my teeth and squeeze my eyes shut. "My dad gave me that when I was ten."

"Blaire—"

No!

I hold up my palm to him. "Just go."

"Let me clean this up—"

"Just go. I got it."

I can't even look at him right now. I know he's frustrated and it was only an accident, but the pain in my chest is only going to get worse if I have to look at him.

He stomps toward his office without another word, and I hang up his jacket and circle my desk to see if anything is salvageable.

The main pedestal and figures of the little girl with her father skating on the lake appear to be intact, but the entire dome is gone, sharp, jagged glass sticking up all the way around the base. It's too dangerous to keep, despite its senti-mental value.

I should never have brought it here.

It would have been safer at home, but having it here helped me make it through the long days. Remembering skating with Dad and the crisp, snow-filled air swirling around us instead of being inside this stuffy office.

Tears trickle down my cheeks as I bend down to scrape up the pieces. I grab the base and brush my fingers over the figurines. "I'm sorry, Dad. He didn't mean to."

But Archie can be like that. When his temper shows, you don't want to be caught in the crossfire.

CHAPTER 8

BLAIRE

My stomach turns as the elevator doors slide open in front of me, and I step out onto the executive floor. After what happened Wednesday afternoon, having Archie away at meetings all day yesterday made it a little bit easier to cope.

I didn't have to see him. I didn't have to listen to him try to apologize again. I was able to come in, see the empty spot on my desk, have a good cry, and then move on with my day without the distraction of him being around.

Without him here, I set up interviews with three florists, four different bakeries for the cake, and talk to three locations. Of course, everything is already booked, but money talks, and when I mentioned who the groom was, they were more than willing to "make it work."

But today's a new day, and he'll be here.

Please don't let it be awkward.

Because I have a lot of work to do—wedding planning

and otherwise—and he has his third and final date with his last woman from the top three.

If she doesn't work out, I can't even imagine what it's going to be like around here or what he'll do.

Probably have an epic meltdown…

Or even worse, he might call his exes again.

I inch across the small waiting area and peek around the corner toward his office. Some mornings, he beats me here, but today, it's empty.

Thank God.

I release a sigh of relief and make my way over to my desk. My focus automatically falls to the spot the snow globe used to sit. Dropping the broken pieces in the trash on Wednesday was like throwing away bits of my own heart.

It was just a material object. Logically, I know it's not something to get upset about, but it's just always reminded me of Dad and of all the good times we had skating at Rocke-feller Center or out on the lake upstate.

The good memories I want to hang onto forever. It's why I brought it to work in the first place. So, I'd have something to enjoy on the bad days.

Now, it's gone. But I push away the tears threatening to form and settle in to start my day, hopefully with a boss who isn't in a shit mood.

The elevator pings, and I stiffen and wait. Archie emerges with a cardboard drink holder and a bag in his hands.

What the heck?

He *never* comes in with coffee. He always, always, always drinks it here—and I'm always the one who brings it to him. His Caribbean-blue eyes meet mine, and he offers me a half-smile.

"Good morning, Blaire." He stops on the other side of my desk and nudges some of the snow globes out of the way to set down the drink carrier, which holds one plain paper cup and one sparkly holiday travel mug.

With a tiny grin, he pulls out the fancy holiday mug and holds it out to me. "White chocolate peppermint mocha, right?" One of his eyebrows rises.

"You know my drink?"

He rubs the back of his neck with his free hand. "So...I was right?"

I nod slowly and take it from him as I examine the cup scene with Santa and his reindeer flying across the snowy landscape. Exactly the one I would've picked if I had been there.

A smile pulls at his lips. "I thought you might like that one."

"I do. Thank you."

What the hell is going on?

Archie has never brought me coffee. Ever. He must feel really bad about what happened the other day.

"I'm—" he looks away for a second like he's nervous. Not a Warren trait. "I'm really sorry about what happened the other day. I was frustrated, and I destroyed something you really cared about because I wasn't in control of myself. I won't ever let that happen again."

He reaches in the bag and pulls out a small box wrapped in sparkly snowflake paper. His eyes meet mine, and he sets it in front of me and waits.

I set down my drink and examine the box. "What's this? I don't want any gifts from you, Archie."

"It's not a gift, really, just trying to make things right."

Trying to make things right? That's impossible.

But I tear into the paper slowly and peel it back to reveal a plain white cardboard box. I glance up at him in question, but he just shrugs.

I pop open the box, glance down inside it, and my breath catches. "Oh, my God. How?"

It's impossible.

My hand trembles as I reach in and pull out the snow globe. *My* snow globe. The dad and the little girl skating across the frozen pond. "How did you find the exact same one?"

The corner of his mouth quirks up. "I didn't. After you left on Wednesday, I dug the base of the one I broke out of your garbage and then called around until I found somewhere that could put on new glass and refill it for you."

The tears pool in my eyes, and one trickles down my cheek.

Oh, God. I can't cry in front of my boss.

I swipe it away and examine the globe. "So, this is my snow globe. The one my dad gave me?"

He nods slowly. "I knew how much it meant to you. So, again, I'm sorry."

I look up at him, his gaze full of concern and something else. He's been paying enough attention to know my drink and how much this meant to me. I never would've thought that from the way he acts or the Warren reputation.

Maybe I've misjudged him.

I clear my throat of the emotion choking me and set down the snow globe. "Thank you. Really, that was above and beyond."

He shrugs nonchalantly. "It's the least I could do."

The shrill ring on the phone on my desk ends the weird moment between us, and I lean forward and pull it from the cradle. "Archimedes Warren's office, how can I help you?"

"I need to talk to Archimedes." Senator Warren's harsh, cool tone sends a chill over me.

"Oh, hello, Senator Warren."

Archie's eyes widen, and he shakes his head.

"Sir, he isn't in this morning, and I'm not sure when he'll be available."

"Tell that ungrateful son of mine that he can't avoid me forever. DC is a short flight away." His annoyance and anger vibrate through the line.

"I will let him know that, sir." I hang up with a sigh.

Archie groans. "What did he say?"

"That you need to stop avoiding him, or he'll fly back from DC to talk to you."

"Shit." He trudges toward his office. "I'm going to call him today."

"Good luck. Don't forget, you have your date with Jessica for lunch."

He freezes and squeezes his eyes closed. "What are the chances of this one being good?"

I shrug. "About as likely as your dad is to stop calling you."

"Fuck. If I didn't have bad luck, I wouldn't have any."

ARCHIMEDES

"I *get it*, Dad." I drop my head to my palm and sigh into the phone.

This conversation is getting tedious.

I've about reached the end of my patience.

"Clearly, you don't, son. Otherwise, you never would have considered doing something so idiotic."

"You didn't leave me much choice, did you? Maybe if you and Grandfather would've thought about this logically, you would've realized that forcing some sort of time limit on this is absolutely absurd."

"We did what had to be done to protect the company and keep it in the family, Archimedes. You may not like it and don't want to believe it, but we did this for you."

I snort a laugh and shake my head. This argument is getting old, fast. "For me? Don't try to sell me that line of bullshit, Dad."

"It's not bullshit. We want this company to be around for a long, long time, and that requires somebody strong and committed at the helm. Artemis did not have what it takes. But you do. We want to make sure you keep your head in the game."

"By forcing me to marry a woman I don't love?"

"Love is overrated, son." His response comes so fast. So final. Like it's not even a question.

I bite back my retort because there's no point in arguing with the old man. There's no point in arguing with a Warren ever. What's done is done. The trust has been changed, and there's no going back.

"I have to go, Father. I have a lunch date shortly."

"With some random woman who applied to be your wife on the internet?"

"Exactly." I hang up before he can say anything else demeaning or insulting.

Even though I intended to call him as soon as I came in this morning, I sat in my office and stared at all the things I needed to get done and just couldn't handle talking to him. I put it off and put it off until there was hardly any time left before my date. I figured calling him right before I knew I had to leave would be a good excuse to cut it short if need be.

I'm glad I did it. Otherwise, I'd be stuck listening to him yell at me for another hour.

Blaire has left me completely alone since I came in here, and I can't tell if she's mad that I pulled the snow globe out of the trash or not. Maybe it was the wrong move. I thought I was doing the right thing by trying to fix what I had broken. But her silence makes me uneasy—almost as much as her laugh has the last week.

I shift in my chair and glance up toward her desk as she rises. The bright-red skirt hugs her hips and ass, and the green sweater with the elf on the front emphasizes her assets on top, too.

Don't stare, Archie. You're being a perv.

She turns and glances over at my office then makes her way toward me. Each step closer she comes, the tighter my chest gets. The woman arriving for this date might be my future wife, and nerves I've never felt before are suddenly invading my body.

Blaire pushes open the door and nods at me. "She's here."

"And?" I raise an eyebrow. I'm just waiting for the list of what's wrong with this one—of what she lied about or what she's hiding. Surely, Blaire will be upfront after the fiasco Wednesday.

But all Blaire does is push her lips together in a firm line and let the door close behind her as she walks back toward her desk.

Nothing to say about this one? That can't be good at all.

I groan and push up from my seat. At least we have a system in place now in case I need to cut this short. I can always text Blaire again and have her give me an excuse to ditch out.

Though if she's mad at me, she might leave me hanging to suffer through another miserable lunch with another miserable woman.

The thought makes me shudder, and I make my way to the small reception area holding my breath. Blaire nods toward the couch, and I turn to face my next suitor.

Holy...wow.

Jessica Sims rises from the couch and offers me a shy smile, her pale green eyes flashing with appreciation. The petite woman with the flowing auburn hair looks exactly like she did in the photo she sent.

Cute. Sweet. Wife material.

Dressed in a conservative skirt, blouse, and kitten heels, she's beautiful and sexy but not overtly so. This is a woman who doesn't try too hard. And I can appreciate that.

I glance over at Blaire and catch a scowl she quickly forces into a smile.

Why is she mad? This one looks promising.

I approach Jessica and offer her my hand. "It's wonderful to meet you."

She accepts my hand in her small one and releases a nervous giggle. "I'm sorry. I'm a little bit nervous. Not really sure what I'm supposed to do."

You and me, both.

There's no rule book for how to find a wife in a month. The fact that she's acknowledging the awkwardness of the situation instead of treating it like a job interview is actually endearing.

I smile, place my other hand on top of hers, and squeeze gently. "Don't worry about it. This is kind of an unusual situation."

Her tinkling laughter floats through the air and bounces off the tile around the reception area. A huff sounds from the direction of Blaire's desk, and I glance over my shoulder at her. She glares at us for a second then focuses her attention on something on her desk.

I turn back to Jessica. "Shall we?"

She nods, and I release her hand and place mine on her lower back to lead her to the elevator. I press the button and glance over my shoulder to find Blaire sitting in her chair with her arms crossed over her chest, looking definitively not happy.

Maybe something happened between them before I came out?

There has to be some reason she looks so pissy.

I don't know how it could be because of this woman, though. This one might just be *the one.*

CHAPTER 9

BLAIRE

"Earth to Blaire."

"Huh?"

Brandy stares at me from across the table and raises her blond eyebrows. "I've been talking to you for five minutes while you just sit there, stirring your drink completely zoned out. Did you hear a word I said?"

I drop my face into my palms and shake my head. "No. I'm sorry. I'm just a little distracted tonight. What were you saying?"

She sighs and waves me off. "Don't worry about it. Wasn't important. What is up with you, anyway? We came out for drinks and dinner to try to have some fun after a long week, but you certainly don't look like you're having any fun right now. Is Archie being a dick again?"

It might be preferable. At least I'd know how to deal with that.

I chuckle and run my hands back through my hair, then take a sip of my white chocolate peppermint martini. "Actually, no. The opposite."

"What do you mean the opposite?"

"Remember how I told you he broke the snow globe my dad gave me on Wednesday?"

She nods slowly. "Yeah."

"Well, apparently, after I left for the night, he took the broken pieces out of my trashcan and spent all night looking for someone who could fix it."

She freezes with her wine glass halfway to her mouth. "What?"

"Yep!" I nod slowly. "And then he showed up this morning with the repaired snow globe and a peppermint white chocolate mocha for me."

"You're fucking kidding." She leans forward, her mouth agape. "Total twilight zone behavior. Are you sure he wasn't body-snatched?"

I chuckle and twirl my glass in front of me, watching the little floating crystals of sugar swirl around. "Maybe he was. I don't really know what's going on with him. It's very unlike Archie to do something so sweet."

"And he knew your drink, too."

"Weird, right?"

A small grin plays at her lips. "He's been paying attention to you. He *likes* you!"

"He does *not!*"

She wiggles her eyebrows. "And you like *him.*"

"What?" I jerk upright. "I do not. At least, not like *that!* He's my boss, and he's a Warren."

"So?"

"So. The man is from one of the wealthiest families in the country. I was born in a trailer park. And I'm *so* not his type."

"How do you know that?"

I huff and cross my arms over my chest, my annoyance from earlier today creeping over my skin. "Because he went on a date with his type earlier today."

"Oh, really? He finally get a date who is decent?"

I chuckle, remembering the fiascoes of Monday and Wednesday. Then acid crawls up my throat, thinking about Jessica today. His reaction to her. My reaction to *his* reaction. I saw the spark there. In his eyes. He likes her. Really likes her. I don't know why it upsets me so much. It's not like we're ever going to be together.

But I still felt a little green.

"You're jealous."

"What?" I drop my mouth open. "I am *not*."

She points a finger at me with a grin. "Yes, you are. You're jealous because you *like* him."

"I do not like him."

She rolls her eyes. "Yeah, okay. Keep lying to yourself."

"I'm not."

Her hand darts out, and she grabs a breadstick, tears off a bite, and chews. "You are. Anyone would be. Archimedes Warren is the most eligible bachelor in New York City. Hell, he's one of the most eligible bachelors in the world, frankly. You'd be crazy not to like him, especially with as much time as you two spend together and have been during this whole planning thing. And now, he's bringing you gifts and making sweet gestures. Admit it, Blaire, you like the guy."

I lean back in my chair and circle my finger around the rim of my glasses as I contemplate her accusation.

Do I?

Of course, I do. How could I not?

Archie can be sweet and generous—and also demanding and annoying—but deep down, he's a good guy, and we both know that.

But I'm also not naïve enough to think anything can ever happen between us.

"Even if I weren't his employee, I'm still not Warren-bride

material. And it doesn't matter, anyway. I have a feeling he hit it off with Jessica today."

"What makes you say that?"

I shrug. "The way he reacted when he saw her. There was a little spark and giggles."

"Archimedes Warren giggled?"

I groan. "Yeah, sort of."

"What about when he got back from lunch?"

I cringe and bite my lip. "I, uh, left early today."

Her eyes widen. "So you wouldn't have to see him! Oh, girl. You have it *bad!*"

"Maybe you're right. But it doesn't matter."

"There's time."

"Time for what?"

She waves her breadstick at me. "Time for him to come to his senses and realize he should be marrying *you.*"

I bark out a laugh so loud, all the tables around us turn and glare at me. I hold up a hand in apology. "That's never going to happen, Brandy."

Only in my dreams.

She shrugs and leans back in her chair. "I don't know, Blaire. You're not just planning the guy's wedding...you're planning *your* wedding. Does he know you're using your wedding book to get this thing organized?"

I sigh and sip my drink. "No. That would be weird. He doesn't need to know that. He just needs things to be taken care of with as little involvement as possible. With this deal hanging over him, he doesn't want to have to make decisions about anything...except the cake."

Her eyebrow wings up. "The cake?"

I chuckle. "Yes, he told me, in no uncertain terms, that I should pick everything and get it booked without worrying about his input, except for the cake. Apparently, the man is very particular about his desserts and wants to taste-test them all."

Brandy rolls her eyes. "Typical man—only cares about the food."

I laugh and finish off my martini. "He cares about a lot of things, Brandy, just not the details of the wedding."

"But you care. Enough that you put all the elements of your dream wedding into that binder when you were a little girl. You don't think it's weird to be using it to plan your boss' wedding?"

"No," I shake my head, "he needs the help. And it's not like I have any marriage prospects on the horizon."

ARCHIMEDES

I take a sip of my bourbon and flip on the television to kill some time before I need to leave. The soft cushions of the couch cocoon me, and if I'm not careful, I may end up passing out.

This week has been so damn exhausting, and it's not even over yet. There hasn't been any time to sleep with all that needs to happen to complete the acquisition...and to plan my wedding. Thank God Blaire is handling basically all the ceremony and reception stuff. There isn't enough time in the day, and even with her help, it's going to be a mad scramble to make sure everything is taken care of.

Of course, Mother and Grandmother offered their assistance, but they're forcing me into a loveless marriage. The last thing I want is their hands in the wedding, too. I'm confident Blaire will arrange a beautiful ceremony my future wife will be happy with. She's never let me down before.

I settle into an episode of *House Hunters*, and my phone rings in my pocket.

Why now?

All I wanted was ten damn minutes to relax. I can't even get that anymore.

I glance down at the screen and sigh. "Artie, what's up?"

"Not much. I just got off the phone with Dad, so I wanted to check in with you to see how you're doing."

I snort and take another sip of my drink. If we're going to talk about Father, then I'm definitely going to need more alcohol in my system. "To say my conversation with him yesterday was tense would be an understatement."

Artemis chuckles. "I have no doubt. I've been there."

He has. And then some.

His conversations with Mother and Father when he reconnected with Penelope and had to tell them about Max weren't comfortable for anyone. And they continue to take out their frustration of that situation on everyone else in the family.

I rub at my tired eyes with my free hand. "What else did he say?"

"He mentioned you had another date yesterday. How did that go?

"Actually," I swirl my drink around the highball glass. "It went really well."

"Really? Nothing wrong with this one?"

I snort and take a sip of my drink. "Everyone has flaws somewhere, Artemis. I just haven't found hers yet."

He laughs. "Give it some time."

"That's one thing I don't have. But lunch was really good. She's from Iowa. Her dad is a state senator. She went to Columbia."

"What's her degree in?"

I snort again. "Get this—public administration. She works for the city."

"Wow. Mom and Dad will love her."

"I know." That should say something about the woman I'm considering marrying, but I'm not entirely sure what.

"So, she's got a great background, a great education that looks good on paper, and you actually like her?"

"I know, right. What are the fucking chances? She's cute and a little bit shy and seems very sweet."

"Then what is she doing answering an ad to be the wife to an asshole like you?"

I set down my drink and squeeze my eyes closed, dropping my head against the back of the couch.

That's the ultimate question, isn't it?

Women don't want to meet their future husbands via classified ad with only three weeks to get to know him before getting hitched. It's not exactly the fairy tale they grow up expecting.

And I tried to analyze that very thing while out on the date with Jessica.

"I think she's just lonely. I got the impression that she has a hard time getting out and meeting people because she isn't very forward and is so shy."

"You think she'll do okay at family events and being in the limelight if she's that shy?"

The question has crossed my mind. I consider it for a moment, again. Once she got comfortable with me at lunch, she was animated and much more open. "I think she'd be okay after a while."

"You're willing to risk that? What if it becomes too much for her and she wants out? You lose the company."

I reach for my drink and take another sip. "Don't remind me. You know it's your fault Father and Grandfather put the stupid clause in the trust in the first place."

He scoffs. "Well, excuse me for following true love."

True love...something I never experienced and probably never will now that I'm stuck in this position.

Jessica was sweet and pretty and would make the perfect Warren bride, but it definitely wasn't love at first sight. Attraction, sure. Lust, not really. But there was a little something there. And maybe it'll just take some time to let that little something grow into something more.

Or...it might never happen, and I'll spend my life in a loveless marriage like Mother and Father.

"So," Artie hums, "are you going to give this girl the ring?"

I scrub a hand over my face and turn to stare out the windows of my place overlooking the city. "We're going out again tonight."

"Two dates in two days? You really must like this girl."

"More like I don't have any time to waste. I need to make a decision and propose fast."

"Are you going to wait until then to start the wedding plans?"

I push to my feet from the couch, grab my drink, and wander over in the kitchen. "I can't. You know what goes into planning a wedding?"

He chuckles. "Yeah, I have some idea, asshole."

Their wedding wasn't huge. In fact, the tiny ceremony on the beach at their house was the opposite of a Warren wedding. It had love and the people they cared about there.

"Well, I now have three weeks to get a New York wedding fit for a Warren planned and to decide on the bride. Thankfully, Blaire is handling most of the wedding plans so I can concentrate on work and the whole bride issue."

"So, this Jessica. What does she look like?"

"Petite, flawless, pale skin, auburn hair, and green eyes."

Artemis laughs, the sound booming through the line.

"What? Why is that funny?"

"You sound like you're describing Blaire."

I freeze. "Huh. I hadn't really thought about it, but she does look a lot like Blaire."

"You know, I always wondered why you never pursued anything with her."

"Are you serious? She's my assistant. That's just asking for a lawsuit if I did that."

He snorts. "You worry too much, Archie. You need to live a little."

"Not if I want to head this company."

Artie releases a heavy sigh. "Work isn't everything, you know. You have to learn to enjoy yourself and take what you want."

"What I want is to be CEO."

"But at what expense?" Someone yells something in the background, and Artie jostles the phone. "Hey, Max is calling for me. I gotta go. Just don't be blinded by Father and Grandfather's demands on you. I don't want to see you miserable for the rest of your life."

He hangs up, and I down the rest of my drink with the wrong green-eyed, red-haired girl in my head.

CHAPTER 10

BLAIRE

"What on earth are you wearing?" Archie stands at the corner of my desk, staring down at me.

I was so engrossed in picking wedding flowers now that I've selected a florist that I didn't even hear him approach. I peek down at my ugly Christmas sweater and back up to the man looking at me as though I've lost my mind.

Though it may look like it, I haven't. I flash him my biggest smile. "What? You don't like it?" I stand up, pushing my chair back from my desk, and sweep my arms along my torso to showcase the gaudy number.

Archie's eyes follow my hands, and everywhere his gaze falls heats, almost like he's physically touching me. It's too intimate for an assistant to be feeling about her boss.

I drop my hands and shake off the inappropriate thought. *It's all in your head, Blaire.*

This man isn't into me in any way, shape, fashion, or form. I'm so far from his type that we're on opposing ends of the spectrum. Maybe I shouldn't listen to Brandy while having drinks. It's putting weird thoughts into my head. Ones I positively shouldn't be thinking.

His azure eyes trace their way across my body and land back on mine. "Um, yeah. It's great?"

I can't contain my laugh at the look on his face, almost like he's in pain while he tries not to hurt my feelings.

Maybe I should cut him some slack.

"Relax. I know it's ugly. It's supposed to be. I'm going to an ugly sweater party tonight at Tavern on the Green. I just thought it'd be fun to wear to work today, too."

Although, despite all its awesome ugliness, I do sort of secretly love it. He doesn't need to know that, though.

"Oh, thank God." He points to the bird. "What is it supposed to be?"

"A partridge in a pear tree." I motion to the partridge. "I bought it online."

The green, pear-shaped tree comes complete with half of a real terracotta pot glued to the sweater for the tree trunk to nestle in. And of course, a fake bird glued to the tree with working Christmas lights, ornaments, bows, and garland.

"Well, it's definitely festive." He hands me his jacket, and our fingers accidentally brush. That same little jolt I've been experiencing the last couple weeks shoots through my system, and our eyes lock.

For a second, I drown in the deep pools of blue. His teeth rake his bottom lip slightly.

Christ, I wonder what his lips taste like?

My tongue darts out across my lips.

Crap.

I whirl toward the coat closet to break the intensity of the moment.

What the hell was that?

Archie clears his throat. "What's in the box?"

I hang up his jacket and turn back to see his eyes laser-focused on a green box resting on the corner of my desk. "Another ugly sweater. I have a blind date tonight for the party. He's going to meet me here. That's for him to wear."

"You have a date? With whom?" His almost accusatory tone gives me pause. He seems a tad perplexed, almost like he's shocked I can get a date.

I cross my arms over my chest, causing the partridge to perch directly on my boob.

Archie tries to hold in his laugh, but he fails miserably.

I uncross my arms, and the partridge returns to its normal resting place, but my irritation hasn't budged. "I can get a date, you know."

His eyes widen, and he holds up his hands. "I never said that you couldn't. I'm just not comfortable with you being on a date with someone you don't know."

What? Hypocrite much? Why would he be worried? More importantly, why would he care?

"I'll be okay. We have a mutual friend who set this up." My comment comes off a little bit more defensive than I intend. After all, he's just concerned with my well-being, right?

But the mutual friend happens to be Matthew's mother, who also happens to be my neighbor. After months of her pestering me to meet her son, I finally relented—partially to get her to stop, and partially because it's been so long since I've been on a date, I was starting to feel like a nun.

Archie doesn't need to know any of that, though. It makes me seem desperate or pathetic or both.

I thought the party tonight would be the perfect date. If things don't work out, at least we aren't trapped awkwardly, alone together at a restaurant.

Archie drops his hands and shrugs. "I just want you to be safe. Dating is hard these days. But at least you get to date, right?"

I bite back the words that hang on the tip of my tongue.

You can date. You do have a choice. You're choosing the wrong path.

How can he not see that?

He could walk away from all of this. He has a great education and work experience. Connections. People start from scratch every day and break away from overbearing families and their expectations.

But I hold those thoughts back because, at the end of the day, Archie is my boss. He's not my friend or anything else, no matter what I may daydream about. His love life, or lack thereof, isn't my business. Not really. Sure, I've been helping him with Operation Find a Wife, but now that he may have potentially identified her and I have the wedding plans well in-hand, my part in his quest has ended.

Eager to get the attention off me and my flop of a personal life, I turn it on him. "Speaking of dates, did your second date with Jessica go well last weekend?"

Even though I ditched out on work early last Friday so I wouldn't have to hear about what I presumed was a wonderful lunch date with Jessica, the office was positively buzzing this entire week about the fact that they went out *again* last weekend.

Two dates mean something considering how the others went.

I've tactfully avoided bringing it up all week, but the curiosity is starting to eat away at me, plus anything to get the focus off me is welcome.

His hand scrubs at the back of his neck. "It was good. I, uh, I think that she is the one."

My chest tightens, and the air escapes my lungs. He's done it, then. He's found her.

Why does that make me want to curl into a ball and cry?

"Really? That's great!" I hope my fake smile makes up for the waver in my voice.

I shouldn't care. I know it's silly, but deep down, a part of me wanted to believe Brandy. That maybe the snow globe could have been more than a kind gesture from an apologetic boss.

"Yeah. I think I will propose, to ah, Jessica, this weekend. Let's hope she says yes." His brow furrows in what I can only describe as confusion before he continues. "Thank you for your help, Blaire. I honestly couldn't have done this so swiftly without you."

"That's great." *It's not.* "I'm so happy to hear that it worked out." *No, I'm not.*

Strangely, the hurt doesn't dissipate.

Why?

It's not like I had a snowball's chance in hell of us becoming anything at all.

So why does this feel like I somehow lost?

He seems to pick up on my mood swing as he slowly turns toward his office, keeping an eye on me, like his psycho Christmas-sweater-wearing assistant may attack him with a snow globe at any moment. "Well, um, thanks again."

"Yep."

He hurries into his office.

Thank God.

Hearing those words…that she is *The Chosen One,* bothers me more than it should. And having Archie hovering around my desk while I prepare for my date is about as awkward as it can get.

ARCHIMEDES

"Blaire, would you get the Ferguson file from legal for me, please."

Her annoyed huff comes through the intercom, but a few seconds later, she replies in her perfectly professional voice, "Yes, sir, Mister Warren."

Sir? Mister Warren? Are we back to this shit now?

She knows I don't want her to call me that. I've expressly asked her not to enough to make it annoying. But maybe since our little side project is over, aside from a few ceremony issues and choosing the cake, she thinks she needs to turn back to a more professional working relationship.

Or, she could just be nervous about her blind date tonight.

Hell, I'm nervous about it.

What if she likes him and they start dating? That'd be good, right?

It should be.

Anyone finding someone they truly connect with and enjoy and want to spend their time with is *good* thing. Yet the thought brings a strange tension to my body.

Really, it isn't any of my business, but from the moment she handed me that bit of info, I've been trying to figure out how to get his last name so I can have security run a check on his ass.

What if he's a creep?

My door flies open, and Blaire marches in, all business.

It's so unlike her, at least unlike *us* in recent weeks. Things have been so relaxed. So...fun.

I don't know what is going on with her, but I don't like it one fucking bit. It's almost quitting time, and we've spent all day with this weird tension.

Did I say something to upset her?

I watch her place the file on my desk. "Ferguson file, sir." She practically throws the words at me, then immediately whirls to head back for the door.

But I'm not having this "sir" bullshit. "Blaire."

She stops in her tracks at my gruff tone but doesn't turn to face me, and I take a moment to appreciate her ass in that black pencil skirt. "We've had this conversation before. Please, call me Archie."

She shakes her head before turning to face me. Her green eyes blaze with a heat that matches the fire-red hair framing her gorgeous face. Even in that fucking atrocious sweater, she's sexy.

My cock pushes against my zipper.

Please, God, don't make me need to stand right now.

Blaire can't see just how much I appreciate her presence.

She smiles, an entirely fake smile, nothing like the genuine ones I've received from her the last few weeks, then shoots me a couple of finger guns. "You've got it, Archie."

I watch her strut back out to her desk.

What in the hell was that?

My ringing cell doesn't let me contemplate our interaction for long. I swipe the call open and lean back in my chair. "Athena. How's California?"

She laughs into the phone. "Sunny. So, how's the wife hunt?"

I'm surprised she waited this long to call and ask. Studying for finals must have her busier than I thought. "Ah, well, I actually found a suitable candidate. Blaire's idea worked. Can you believe it?"

"Really?" The genuine shock in her voice floats through the line. "You're seriously going through with this?"

"What other choice do I have? I *have* to do this."

Athena sighs like she's exhausted every bit of patience she has. And that's probably true. She definitely didn't inherit the Warren ability to maintain a façade. Keeping her true feelings in isn't her forte at all.

I rub at my throbbing temple. "I plan to propose to Jessica this weekend."

"You know, for someone so smart, you really are dense. I hope you realize what you truly need before it's too late. We'll talk soon."

The line goes dead, and I look at my phone like it holds the answers to what in the world my sister means.

Too late for what?

Athena loves being obtuse, but I don't have time to wonder about it for long. The Ferguson file needs attention, and I get lost in it for what feels like hours.

By the time I look out the window, daylight has slowly slipped away, replaced by the inky blackness of the crisp evening. Streetlights from below our building cast an eerie glow against the window.

The Ferguson file can come home with me tonight to review this weekend. I can't sit in here anymore tonight. I'll need to look at some of their assets to see if they warrant the hefty investment from Warren Enterprises, but the decision can wait until Monday.

When I first moved into this office after Artemis left, it was like a dream. Tonight, it feels stifling.

The clock on the edge of my desk says it's past six.

Why didn't Blaire tell me she was leaving?

She always checks in at five to see if I need anything else before she heads home for the day.

She must be upset with me about something.

Apparently, having your assistant help you in your matrimonial quest makes for awkwardness after the search is over. Maybe it wasn't the best idea to rely so heavily on her, but it's not like I have some sort of handbook for how to handle this type of situation.

Hopefully, she'll be back to normal on Monday. I don't want things awkward like this forever.

I shove the file into my briefcase and head for the door to my office but stop in my tracks.

Why is Blaire still here?

She sits at her desk, back to me.

"Blaire, what are you still doing here?"

She should have been long gone. I guess Matthew doesn't believe in being prompt when a beautiful woman is waiting for him.

Figures.

I knew I didn't like this dickhead from the second she mentioned his name.

Blaire doesn't answer me. She just sits at her desk, an elbow resting on the surface, her fist tucked under her chin. Her other hand rests on her lap on top of the box containing the sweater Matthew was supposed to wear.

What happened to him?

She looks dejected, and after the way she acted toward me today, I'm not sure that I'm not somehow partly to blame for the furrow marring her beautiful brow.

She sighs heavily. "He didn't show up. He didn't call, either. I guess I got stood up."

The disappointment lacing her words is like a knife stabbing at my gut.

You're an asshole, Matthew.

But part of me is just a little bit relieved that he is.

"Oh, I'm sorry, Blaire. So, you're not going to go to the party? You're just going to go home?"

She shakes her head. "No, it's a party thrown by my best friend's work. I go every year. I'm still going to go. I guess I'll just be going alone."

Shit.

The thought of her going alone brings another pang of something.

This tension that's hung between us all day needs to dissipate, and I also can't stand to see her disappointed over this dipshit, Matthew.

She rises from her chair and gathers her things before tucking the box under her arm.

A little levity might lighten the mood. "Maybe your date didn't show up so he didn't have to wear that ugly sweater." I bark out a laugh, but she isn't laughing with me.

Well, shit. That backfired.

She probably thinks I'm laughing *at* her, not the damn sweater.

"Good night, Archie. Have a good weekend." She walks around me, headed toward the elevator without a backward glance in my direction.

"Blaire, I was joking."

She stops long enough to toss the box into the trash before she pushes the button to summon the elevator. The doors slide open, and she turns to face me.

What I see nearly breaks my heart. Blaire's really upset, more so than I even realized. Instead of being a good friend to her like she has been for me the last few weeks, I made her feel worse.

Fuck, I made fun of something she was excited about.

I'm an asshole.

"Blaire."

The doors shut, and the elevator descends.

"Fuck!" I rush over and slam my hand against the button as if that will bring her back up to me.

I can't believe I made her feel worse.

How the hell do I fix this?

CHAPTER 11

BLAIRE

Two things are abundantly clear:

Archie is an ass, and I am really, really buzzed.

In the hour since I arrived at the party, I've been drowning my sorrows in a steady stream of booze.

It's pathetic, really.

I'm too old to get drunk to try to comfort myself. But it is what it is. After the last few hours on top of an equally crazy week, I needed an escape.

And I'll pay for this tomorrow.

But still, I can't believe Matthew stood me up. My mercy date was a no show. How ironic. Maybe I was a mercy date for him, as well.

God, that's really, really pathetic.

I down the rest of the green concoction and tap the empty glass on the bar top. "Hit me, bartender. Another Grinch!"

Brandy grabs my arm. "That was your third Grinch in an hour. I think we need to slow the party bus down, Blaire."

I frown at her. "I have had a rough week. Work was crazy busy, and oh, get this...my hot boss is getting married to a stranger I hand-picked for him. Did you know that?" The combination of all the alcohol and the din of music and multiple conversations taking place around us means what should have stayed private comes out more like a shout, but I don't care. "He's so handsome and maddening and...and mean!" I point at Brandy. "Then, my asshat blind date stood me up. I didn't even want to go out with this guy, you know? I really didn't. I wasn't into it, but I agreed anyway."

The bartender stands a few feet away, talking with a group of ladies who can't seem to make up their mind on their order. "Get a Grinch!" I shout, trying to be helpful but also hurry this along.

I need a refill.

Brandy opens her mouth to interrupt, but I hold up a hand to stop her. I'm on a roll, and the buzz in my veins means there is no longer any filter.

"I thought to myself, *Blaire, give it a shot.* You never know what could happen. It's the season of miracles after all, right? Anything is possible!"

I used to think so, anyway.

Dad always said that anything can happen around Christmas, but this year it seems like it's just punching me in the gut.

I wobble in my heels just a bit, but Brandy catches my arm to steady me.

It should be a sign to stop my drinking and my rant, but I can't seem to rein it in.

"If that wasn't bad enough, Archie just *had* to be there to witness my humiliation. It was so embarrassing."

God, the look on his stupid beautiful face when he realized he'd hurt me as the elevator door closed. Pity? Remorse?

I wanted to punch him and kiss him at the same time. "He

made fun of my sweaters, Brandy. How could anyone make fun of my love for Christmas?" I pout, sticking out my bottom lip. "Archie did. You know why?" I throw my finger in the air as it dawns on me.

It all makes sense now, or maybe, it's just all the alcohol in these Grinches catching up to me.

The irony of my drink of choice tonight isn't lost on me.

"Archie is a Grinch! He hates anything that makes me happy! He even acted surprised that I had a date tonight. I can get a date. I'm not entirely hideous, or well, I thought that was true. Jokes on me though, huh?" I sigh at how pathetic I sound, even to my own ears.

And that damn bartender *still* hasn't come over.

"How can you deny me this?" I tap my glass again.

The bartender's head turns my way, so I shake my glass at him. "Hey, buddy. I need this!"

Brandy pushes my arm down. "Blaire, I'm sorry you're upset, but is it really because this stranger stood you up?"

No, no, it's not.

She sighs and continues, "Or is it because of something else. More like *someone* else. Perhaps like your boss?"

I shake my head vigorously. "No. It has *nothing* to do with Archimedes Warren."

Not his beautiful eyes or handsome face. Not even the jolt that runs through my body at the slightest touch from him. No, not at all. It's not this stupid unrequited crush.

Nope. Definitely not.

"It's been a tough week," I mumble.

I can't even figure out exactly why I'm this upset. It's not like me to let anything having to do with a guy throw me so much.

Surely, it's just typical work stress, right?

Shit, who am I kidding?

Archie is a part of why I'm feeling sorry for myself

tonight, but I'll only let him be a very small part because no matter what I may think or feel toward my boss, he is a lost cause.

There's nothing, not one thing that will ever come from this crush. Brandy looks over my shoulder, then her focus returns to me, and a huge smile appears on her lips. "So, you don't care about Archie? Not at all? Even if he were here, right now, you wouldn't be concerned in the slightest?"

"No. I definitely would not."

She drops her head back and laughs.

"What the hell is so funny? It's not like he'd ever show up to this type of party, anyway." I wave my hand around at everyone dressed in ugly sweaters, each as wonderfully hideous as the next.

This isn't his vibe at all.

Brandy grabs my arm and squeezes. "Blaire, look at the door."

I turn my head, and the empty Grinch glass I've been clinging to for dear life slips from my hand. *Oh, my God!*

"Is that…is that who I think it is?"

Archie stands at the door, scanning the room, mostly blocked from my view by the crowd of revelers.

Is he here for me?

That doesn't make any sense. He thought this whole thing was stupid.

But the crowd parts, and I finally see him…and what he's wearing.

"Oh, my God, Brandy. He's here! And he's wearing an ugly sweater!"

Not just *any* ugly sweater, either.

My heart stalls in my chest.

My ugly sweater.

❄

ARCHIMEDES

Blaire stands at the bar, looking flustered and beautiful in her ugly-ass sweater, with a blonde who must be her friend. They both watch me make my way toward them—her friend wears an amused smile while Blaire's jaw is practically on the floor.

For some reason, butterflies dance in my stomach. Something I haven't felt since I was in the school spelling bee and knew I hadn't prepared.

Why the hell am I nervous?

This is Blaire. I know Blaire. Up until earlier today, we were comfortable with each other. We had a friendship. Something easy and relaxed.

Her eyes lock with mine, then drift down to my sweater. Her lips twitch with a smile that brings out my own.

That smile makes this stupid sweater worth wearing.

"Hey," I slide in beside her at the bar, "nice sweater."

Blaire watches me, and she doesn't exactly seem happy to me, despite the smile she just gave me. "What are you doing here, Archie?"

Straight to the point.

I guess I deserve that.

"Blaire, I didn't mean to upset you. I'm sorry. Can you forgive me for being, um—"

"An ass." She jumps right in. "You were an ass, Archie."

A laugh bubbles from my chest. She's adorable when she's right. "Yeah, I was. I'm sorry."

She considers me for a moment, and her slightly hazy eyes seem to lose some of the anger they just held. "Buy us a Grinch, and I'll let it slide."

"A grinch?" I raise an eyebrow. "Do I even want to know?"

She grins. "No. Probably not."

All it took to make her happy and smile was put on this

stupid sweater and show up. That makes a warmth spread through my chest, and without thinking, I grab her hand where it rests on the bar and intertwine our fingers.

Sparks zing through my body from her touch.

Shit.

We both look at where our fingers interlock, then meet each other's gazes.

Jesus, what am I doing?

I jerk my hand away and turn to look for the bartender. "Uh, Grinches are on me."

An awkward minute lingers where the rush of noise around us fills the air. I clear my throat, trying to brush off the fact that holding her hand felt natural, right, and that I want to do it again.

What the hell is happening?

I force myself to turn back to face Blaire and incline my head toward the blonde. "Who's your friend?"

Blaire shakes off a stunned look and motions toward the girl beside her. "Oh, where are my manners? Brandy, this is Archie. Archie, this is my best friend, Brandy."

Brandy smiles, nudges Blaire, and winks at her. "I like your sweater, Archie."

I look down and chuckle at the absurdity of what I'm wearing. "This old thing?" I pull at the collar, sending the bells on the knitted sweater jingling.

"Well," Brandy scans the room, "it was nice to meet you, Archie. I need to go say hello to someone." She glances at Blaire. "So, I'll see you later?"

Blaire tugs on Brandy's hand, seemingly desperate to keep her here, but her friend just brushes her off and hurries over to a group of people on the far side of the bar. I fight another chuckle as Blaire releases a deep sigh before she turns to face me.

God, she's beautiful.

I mean, I always thought so, but in a *she's-off-limits* kind of way. Getting involved with an employee is a line I can't cross. But right here, right now, my morals feel like they're slowly slipping away...because all I can think about is kissing her.

The bartender makes his way toward us, breaking this spell I seem to be under. "What can I get for you?"

"Two Grinches, please."

He nods and returns a moment later with two glasses of some unknown green concoction.

I take a sip. Definitely boozy but not bad.

If this is what Blaire has been drinking since she arrived, it would explain the slight haze in her eyes. I take a bigger sip. Maybe one of these will help me feel less embarrassed in this damn sweater.

"So, why are you here?" Blaire's point-blank question makes me freeze with the glass against my lips.

I lower it to the bar and turn to face her. Her mane of sunset-red hair flows around her.

What would it look like spread out on my pillows?

Shit.

I shake my head and glance down at the Grinch.

What is wrong me? What's in this drink?

After the last few weeks, I'm not certain I even care and swallow another mouthful. "Blaire, you've been a big help to me the last few weeks. This is the least that I can do to show you how much I appreciate you."

She sips her drink, and a droplet escapes. I reach up and swipe against her plump bottom lip with my thumb before I can even consider what I'm doing.

A tiny gasp floats from her at my touch, and I freeze.

What the hell am I doing?

I need to get a grip, away from her for a minute. "I'm going to go to the bathroom. I'll be right back." The words rush out in one long string of syllables. I can't get away fast enough.

"O-okay."

I make a hasty exit and beeline for the bathrooms.

Something is seriously wrong with me.

I can't seem to keep my hands off Blaire, and that is very, very bad news. I'm going to propose to another woman this weekend and be married at the end of the month. The last thing I should be doing is feeling *anything* for Blaire other than appreciation.

But she has me rattled enough not to watch where I'm going when I round the corner. I smack right into Wayne Ferguson.

Shit. What's he doing here?

Warren family friends aren't usually the type of people who attend ugly sweater parties. And given his outfit, he's not here for it. He's probably entertaining clients in the main dining room or having dinner with his wife.

His eyes widen when he turns to see who slammed into him. "Archie, how are you, and what in the hell are you wearing?"

I don't even bother looking down at the sweater, just release a sigh. The green eyesore decked out with red bows and actual peppermints is bad enough, but to make matters worse, red and white lettering announces *"Jingle My Bells"* down the length of my torso. And the true icing on the humiliation cake is the large red bow and bells dangling from ribbon that hangs right over my cock.

Of all the people to see while I'm wearing this outrage to clothing, it has to be the man whose company I'm trying to buy.

I force a smile and shake Wayne's hand. "I'm doing well. Just here for an ugly sweater party."

Looking completely unprofessional. Not how I ever want a client to see me.

Christ, this is humiliating.

Wayne examines my sweater again and chuckles. "Ah, I see. Only love could make a man go out dressed like that."

"Actually, I'm here with my secretary." I rub the back of my neck, my discomfort growing by the moment. And what I just said made the entire situation even worse.

I just made it sound like I'm having an affair with Blaire.

His bushy white eyebrows rise. "*Really*? She must be great at her job!" He winks and nudges me with his elbow.

I off an uncomfortable laugh. "No, no, it's nothing like that. She's just been extremely helpful at work the last few weeks."

"I bet she has." He leans in to whisper in my ear, "The shit men do for pussy. Am I right?"

Archie, do not punch this man. Do not.

I fist my hands at my sides to keep from slamming one into his face. "Wayne, it's not like that, at all. I'm actually about to get engaged."

He stops laughing for a moment, then seems to consider his words before he leans in again. "Look, Archie, I like you. I think you're smart. I've worked with your grandfather and father on a few projects throughout the years. I can tell you're a chip off the old block. It's why I agreed to continue to work with your company as you transition to CEO."

Over the years, the Fergusons have been major clients and business allies for the Warrens, and the fact that Wayne trusts me to step in as CEO takes some of the concern about the acquisition going through off my shoulders. With no heirs and retirement on the horizon, the sale would make him billions and give us another leg up.

He pauses to glance around, but apparently, he's convinced no one is listening because he leans in again.

"But...your family has certain asinine expectations where your personal life is concerned. I've heard the chatter."

Of fucking course, he knows of my predicament.

It seems everyone does. Stupid trust is ruining my life on every front.

"Look, Wayne, I'm sure you've heard about my situation, but I can assure you that it will not interfere with any business dealings, including this acquisition."

"Son," he places a hand on my shoulder, "I never assumed that it would, but that's not what I'm worried about."

It's not?

I shake my head. "Then, I'm afraid that I don't know what you're talking about."

"A man doesn't wear that," he points to my sweater, "if he doesn't have some sort of feelings. I think you might be missing something about your current situation."

Wait a minute...

"You think I have feelings for my secretary?"

I don't.

Do I?

No.

Of course, not.

I came to this party because...

Shit.

I pulled this thing out of the garbage and wore it because I couldn't stand seeing her so distraught and felt bad that I had played a part in it.

Would I have done that for any employee?

Wayne chuckles and squeezes my shoulder. "As a man who married his secretary thirty years ago, I don't think, son. I know."

I gulp thickly against my suddenly dry throat but am saved from having to respond when Wayne turns to greet someone.

Hell.

I head back toward the bar, the conversation we just had lingering in my mind. Maybe I'm attracted to Blaire...and that's okay. She's smart, funny, and gorgeous.

What man wouldn't be?

I *definitely* don't have feelings for her, though. Not beyond an appreciation for everything she's doing to help ensure I can be CEO.

She comes into view where I left her at the bar, and I laugh, watching her dance with her drink in hand, not a care in the world. Her lithe body rolls to the beat, her fiery hair flowing around her.

With her back to me, she's completely oblivious to my approach, so I take the moment to enjoy her curves as she shimmies and glides to the music.

Fuck it. Fuck what people think. Fuck what my family thinks.

Tonight, I'm living in the moment and am actually going to celebrate a holiday joyfully for once. I'm not going to worry about expectations, familial obligations, business deals, or wives. No, tonight I'm going to have fun with the woman who is basically my only friend except Artie.

I slide up behind her and wrap my arm around her waist, the feel of her warm, tight body pressed against mine sending shivers through me.

She stills instantly, and I lean in to whisper in her ear.

"You want to dance?"

CHAPTER 12

BLAIRE

His whispered words send goose bumps skittering across my skin, and at the same time, my entire body heats, like I'm standing in the center of a blazing inferno.

Maybe it's the Grinches.

His grip tightens around me, and I have to clench my thighs to keep from telling him I'm more interested in a horizontal dance.

Too many Grinches, for sure.

"Yes." The single word comes out on a shaky breath.

The rumble of his laughter vibrates against my neck, sending lust coursing through my veins. I squeeze my eyes shut, and he slides his hand across my waist and down my thigh to grab my hand. Before I melt into a puddle right in front of the bar, he leads me toward the dance floor.

I'm about to dance with my boss.

It's simultaneously the most exhilarating and terrifying prospect in the world.

Archie twirls me around the floor, then pulls me close. All

I can do is smile like a lunatic, the boozy Grinches doing away with any inhibition I may have had.

We sway side to side effortlessly, our bodies melded together like they're meant to be that way, moving in time with the slow, sensual song playing. It's easy to forget where we are, all the people surrounding us, when we're like this. It's easy to think about things that are far too dangerous to be considering.

What would being with Archie be like?

I bet he's attentive and would never miss an anniversary. He's a man of details. He never forgets an appointment, a name, a fact. He knows more about his workday than I do, and I'm the one who's paid to keep up with it.

And after what he did for me tonight, donning this sweater I know he thinks is absolutely ridiculous, I'm confident he would treat me like a queen.

I rest my head on his chest, close my eyes, and sway back and forth to the beat of the music.

Was Brandy right? Did the snow globe mean more than I'm willing to acknowledge?

I inhale the wonderful scent that's all Archie—leather and spice—and listen to his heart beating in time with the music.

His left hand strokes my lower back softly, barely even brushing my skin. But I'm more aware of that touch than anything I've ever experienced in my life. Every nerve ending fires, centered on the place where his fingers flit over my back.

He squeezes my hand tenderly and leads us flawlessly across the dance floor. Of course, he can dance. I shouldn't be surprised, but the effortless way he moves is impressive, nonetheless.

The sereneness of being here in his arms almost washes away all the distress of the week, but all too soon, the song ends, and a more upbeat tempo begins to play.

"Let's get something to drink." He twirls me again and leads me off the dance floor toward the bar with his hand in mine.

I can't stop grinning like a total idiot. "I had no idea you can dance so well."

It's impressive. And sexy as hell.

"Ah, Miss Hall, I have many tricks up my sleeves." He wiggles his eyebrows and squeezes my hand.

A laugh bursts from deep in my chest.

I have no doubt about that.

And I wish I could blame this ethereal feeling on the Grinches, but really, I'm just positively giddy. It's utterly ridiculous, but I can't stop the smile on my lips.

Archie showed up for *me* tonight.

Who the hell knows what that means? If it even means anything at all?

The only thing I'm sure of is that I'd be lying if I said I wasn't happy to see him.

"Did you want another Grinch?" The deep timbre of his voice washes over me.

It momentarily steals my ability to string together words, so I nod. He releases my hand to pull out his wallet to pay the bartender. The sudden loss of his touch immediately dampens my mood.

I don't want to consider what that means. Or how *wrong* it is.

Thinking about anything other than how amazing it felt to be in his arms can wait until tomorrow—when reality comes crashing back down and I'm hungover from these monster-green drinks.

He holds another one up toward me. "One Grinch. Maybe you should have some water after this one."

I flash him my most devious grin. "It's a Christmas party,

Archie. Nothing wrong with being festive. Besides, I didn't drive."

He hands me the drink, and I take a generous sip. The interesting mix of flavors dances across my tongue, and almost instantly, the alcohol warms me.

Someone bumps into my back, and I glance around. The party is so packed tight, it's almost stifling.

I motion toward one of the patio doors. "Let's step outside and get some air, you want to?"

"That sounds good." He takes my hand again and leads me toward the door to the outside dining area.

A group of people stand around the door, and as we approach it, they chant, "Kiss, kiss, kiss."

What are they talking about?

I glance around us to see if I'm missing something and then turn back to Archie. He shrugs, apparently just as clueless as I am.

One of the women in the group points up above the door where mistletoe hangs, now directly above our heads.

Oh. My. God.

Our gazes snap together—his blue eyes darkening the longer they're locked on mine. My stomach twists, and I try to pull my hand out of his.

I never would have suggested going out this way if I'd known. Kissing my boss would be a very, very bad idea. "Archie, we don't have to, really."

The words barely leave my lips before Archie's arm wraps around my waist, and he drags me up against him.

His mouth twists into a heart-stopping grin. "It's tradition."

Before I can even take another breath, his lips land on mine.

❄

ARCHIMEDES

I press my lips to the pillowy softness of Blaire's. A tiny little moan slips from her mouth into mine, the sound alone enough to fuel my need for more.

More of kissing her. More of her lips. More of *her.*

Christ, her mouth.

I could kiss her endlessly and never tire of it. Thankfully, the loud music conceals my groan because letting Blaire know how much I'm really enjoying this when I'm very publicly planning a wedding to another woman—with her help—would be all sorts of wrong. But even knowing that, I can't drag myself away. Instead, I brush my fingers against her jaw and angle myself for better control.

My tongue glides along the seam of her lips, begging for entrance, and she opens for me.

Thank fuck.

If she denied me now, if she took the time to consider what's happening and the circumstances that make this so wrong, she might stop, and I don't know how I would tear myself away from her taste or touch.

Our tongues battle—swirling and thrusting—and everyone and everything happening around us disappears.

I want for nothing but for this moment to last, to revel in the feeling of having her in my arms and tasting her with each breath. Her arms wrap around my neck, and I pull her impossibly closer.

Kissing Blaire is like tasting freedom.

It's everything I want. A beautiful, intelligent, fun woman who's interested in me for me. Not for my name, not for my money. Not for what any of that can bring her.

I haven't even kissed Jessica yet and can already tell it won't be like this. Even if we develop the kind of connection and friendship Blaire and I have, I'll always wonder what her true motives are, what lies beneath the pleasant, shy smile and care she shows me.

How will I ever know what's real?

With Blaire, I know.

This is real.

This moment we shouldn't be sharing.

She nips my bottom lip, and I groan, my cock approving of her oral skills. I adjust my stance to keep my growing interest from interrupting the fucking fantastic kiss.

Fuck.

I'm kissing Blaire.

I'm kissing my assistant, Blaire.

My tongue is in my secretary's mouth.

Fuck. I'm kissing the hell out of Blaire!

What the hell was in those Grinches?

I can't say I don't enjoy the press of her body against mine. Truthfully, I've imagined it more than once recently, as completely inappropriate as it might be. And the reality is far better than anything I ever could have dreamed up.

Her hands twine into the back of my hair, and she tugs slightly, eliciting another groan and making me squeeze her tighter.

I'm definitely liking this side of Blaire. I never imagined kissing her would be this way. Hell, I didn't even consider it a possibility. All the time we've spent together to find a suitable wife has brought us closer than I thought possible. Closer than is probably wise.

Who knew that beneath that gaudy Christmas sweater lurked a feisty, sexual woman waiting to be brought out?

Her small hand grips my ugly sweater. Her touch sends my heart racing and my mind soaring with possibilities.

Pointless possibilities because this, us...she and I can never be. Something a huge part of me wishes weren't true.

But it's reality, Archie.

Mustering up as much willpower as I can, I force myself to pull away, then go back for another last peck.

God, her kisses are like a drug.

I stroke her cheek, and she leans into my touch.

"Blaire." Her name escapes my lips on a sigh, and I shake away the fog this moment has brought over my mind.

She looks at me dreamily with those forest-green eyes, and I get lost in her, in this moment, again. I lean in one last time and sweep my mouth against hers softly.

This is the last woman I'll ever get to kiss before my marriage. In a few weeks, it'll be a virtual stranger's lips on mine.

Will she make me feel like Blaire is at this moment?

I can only hope. But something tells me this spark and feeling is all Blaire.

Her small hand brushes my cheek, and I want to devour her, but I don't. Because this is Blaire, my friend, my employee, and inviting her home with me would be vastly unfair to her no matter how much I may want to.

I pull away, and the loss of her warmth hits me immediately. Like moving from the sun into an ice bath. I stare at her beautiful face and try to regain my bearings.

"Okay, let's grab some air, shall we?" I smile at her and push open the door, but Blaire stands stock still. "Blaire?"

Shit. Have I ruined our friendship with my inability to control myself?

Her uncertain gaze darts between my face and the door. "Yeah, um, I actually need to go find Brandy."

What? Okay.

I scrape my hand through my hair and sigh. She can't wait to get away from me. Maybe I took things too far.

Did I misread the situation? We were having fun. Weren't we?

I allow the heavy metal door to close, the sound symbolic, reminding me that a door has closed on my personal life and any ability I may have had to pursue anything I want in it. "Okay, Blaire. I'll come with you."

I'm not about to abandon her tonight or let her run away and let things get weird between us. I take her hand and guide us back into the fray.

I have to see this moment for what it was. Nothing more than a small escape from my looming realty.

CHAPTER 13

BLAIRE

The doors slide open, and I take a deep, fortifying breath before I step out of the elevator.

With the strap of my shoulder bag clutched in a white-knuckled death grip, the click of my heels against the hard tile brings me closer to my desk but doesn't help dispel my unease.

I've been a wreck since the kiss with Archie on Friday night. It's all I can think about. The entire weekend, I've been wondering what would happen when I came into the office this morning.

Mostly though, I thought about how damn good the man can kiss. Considering his reputation, I didn't expect anything less, but I never anticipated the lingering effects. I touch my lips as if I can still feel the softness, the press of his mouth there.

His kiss has been a phantom that's haunted me all weekend.

I approach my desk and breathe a sigh of relief because,

thankfully, Archie's office remains dark. He'll be here eventually, but at least I have a moment to try to compose myself. I pull out my chair and take a seat before tucking my bag away in the drawer of my desk.

My eyes immediately land on the snow globe Archie had restored for me. I reach out and touch it. It's absolutely pristine. Like nothing ever happened to it. I still can't believe he did that.

And what happened on Friday is just one more thing that has added to my confusion over what is happening between Archie and me.

He kissed me with such passion, such desire. No way was that forced. That wasn't done out of any sense of necessity because of the stupid mistletoe.

Maybe it was due to temporary insanity.

The wife hunt, the party, the Grinches…

Good grief…the Grinches.

The people shouting for him to kiss me, that damn mistletoe—all led to disaster.

I'm certain he felt sorry for me after I was stood up. It was a pity kiss. He regretted it the second our lips parted. The look on his face said as much. Then he popped a few quick pecks to my mouth so I wouldn't *think* it was a pity kiss.

And now, I have no freaking idea how we should handle this situation. We definitely need to discuss it. I don't want any awkwardness between us and playing drunken tonsil hockey with my boss definitely lands us smack dab in the middle of the awkward zone.

With a sigh, I fire up my computer and wait for it to load. Before I can lose myself in what is sure to be a mass of emails, the elevator pings, the doors open, and Archie strolls out, looking absolutely delicious in a charcoal-gray three-piece suit.

His Italian loafers carry him and his hotness ever closer to my desk, and I hold my breath. He zeroes in on me with laser focus.

What is he going to say to clear up this newfound gray zone our relationship drunkenly fell into a few days ago?

He gives me a cool, confident Warren smile. "Good morning, Blaire."

His voice caresses my name, and I have to clear my throat to get myself under control as his spicy scent envelops me. I instantly flashback to being wrapped in his arms, pressed tight against every hard plane of his body as he kissed me senseless.

Did it get hot in here?

"Good morning, Archie."

"How was your weekend?"

Confusing? Stressful? Too damn fast, for sure.

"Good, thanks, and yours?" I smile as he takes off his coat and hands it to me to hang in the closet like this is just any other Monday.

"Very busy. I need the Lancaster files. Would you please grab those from legal for me? I need to get up to date on that before my meeting after the new year with Elaina Lancaster regarding her late husband's company."

"O...kay."

That's it? He doesn't have anything else to say? Nothing about what happened on Friday?

Maybe he isn't comfortable having this talk so publicly, but I'm pretty sure we are the only ones at work this early today, and given that it's Christmas week, most of the office will be empty anyway.

"Thanks, Blaire." With those parting words, he heads through the frosted-glass door of his office.

What was that?

He's acting like nothing happened this weekend. We had

a few too many drinks, but not so many that I can't remember that kiss and the weight of his body against mine—and the fact that, no matter how he tried, he utterly failed to conceal the reaction my touch stirred within his body.

I turn to hang his coat in the closet and then call the legal department to bring up the file. While I wait, the absurdity of his actions this morning occupies my mind.

Is he just going to ignore what happened between us on Friday? He wouldn't. Would he?

The elevator dings, and Tina from legal hustles over with the Lancaster file. "Here you go. Let me know if he needs anything else."

"I will." And now I have to go into his office to give this to him.

Surely, now that we're alone, he'll want to discuss what transpired.

I knock on the frosted glass door to his office and hold my breath.

"Come in." His invitation comes cold and emotionless.

I push open the door and find him leaning back in his chair, looking calm, cool, and collected while I'm an awkward hot mess of nerves and self-doubt. "The Lancaster files, sir."

He quirks an inky brow at me, and for a moment, I can't contain my laugh at my nervous mistake.

"Sorry, Archie."

"Thank you, Blaire."

I hand him the file, and he opens it on his desk and buries his head in the paperwork.

Huh. That's it?

Nothing more to say? He's just going to ignore the very awkward thing standing here between us, begging to be addressed? He's just going to pretend it didn't happen? Pretend his tongue wasn't in my mouth and that his hard dick wasn't pressed up against the terracotta pot glued to my sweater?

"Blaire?" Archie stares up at me with a raised eyebrow. "Was there something you needed?"

Really?

I guess we're going to pretend it never happened.

Okay, then.

I force a smile. "Nope. I'll just see myself out."

And return to my desk more confused than ever.

ARCHIMEDES

Blaire exits, and the door to my office shuts behind her. I breathe a sigh of relief. I thought ignoring what happened between us last Friday would be for the best and would also be the easiest course of action. Far easier than having to look her in the eye and actually discuss it...or even worse, what it might have meant.

Because I can't *let it* mean anything.

Especially since I'm about to propose to Jessica. I was *supposed* to do it this weekend, but after that kiss with Blaire, I just couldn't bring myself to pop the question.

There's still time, though...

I can propose at the Christmas Eve party later this week. It's really the perfect time and location. Surrounded by all the family friends and company clients, Mother and Father won't be able to berate me for stealing their thunder or for finding a wife in this unusual method. They'll have to smile and clap and sip a champagne toast to next week's nuptials just like everyone else.

So, Thursday night, I'll be engaged. And next Thursday, I'll be married.

In the meantime, I just need to push what happened with Blaire out of my head and pretend like her lips and body were never pressed against mine. I just didn't realize it would be this damn difficult and awkward.

Our usual relaxed and sometimes playful rapport has vanished, leaving the morning tense and uncomfortable.

It should be a sign that what I did was a horrible idea. It should confirm I'm doing the right thing by pretending it didn't happen, yet I've made up excuse after excuse just to call her into my office or go to her desk.

Any excuse to be near her.

Requesting unwanted files, coffee, faxes, copies, supplies.

I'm finally out of excuses.

But I can't get her out of my head. Not when her scent lingers in my office from when she brought my third cup of unwanted coffee this morning. Not when that red dress she's wearing with golden embroidered Christmas trees along the bottom of the hem, hugs her every delicious curve, taunting me.

It's all so enticing, even though my lack of acknowledgment of our current situation has only seemed to spurn her wrath. I'd like to think a better man wouldn't be so turned on by her anger and annoyance, but I never claimed to be any such thing.

Seeing her so worked up is getting *me* worked up in a wholly inappropriate way.

That woman can't occupy my mind any longer. Nothing can come of this newfound desire for my assistant.

The days are ticking off the calendar faster than I'd like to acknowledge. It's time I seal the deal with Jessica and put everyone involved out of their misery, even though it means inserting myself right into mine.

Jessica is beautiful, intelligent, kind. She has the perfect job and ideal background to be a wife to a Warren. She's a catch by anyone's standards. She's just not a certain fiery redhead who seems to occupy all my attention the last few weeks.

But that's a fantasy that must remain in the past.

Time to put this crush behind me and move on with my life.

Eye on the prize, Archie.

Soon, the company will be mine. My future at the helm of what Grandfather and Father built will be secured the moment Jessica and I say I do—assuming I manage to knock her up almost right away. At the end of the day, that's what matters most to me—this seat. This job. If I have to take on a bride to get all of it, then so be it.

It's time to accept my fate and stop acting like a child with a crush. Because that isn't reality.

A wedding on New Year's Eve is.

The wedding Blaire is planning…

Christ, that's fucked up.

I rub my hands over my face, and when I look back up, my door opens, and Blaire enters. It's probably a good thing I didn't see her coming. If I had, I would have watched the way her hips sway when she walks. I would have obsessed over the bounce of her curled hair and her soft, creamy skin.

Shit.

Stop it, Archie.

I sit back in my chair, steepling my fingers under my chin.

"Yes, Blaire? What do you need from me?"

A good fuck right here on my desk comes to mind.

Her eyes flash with the restrained heat of her anger—or maybe it's attraction. It's certainly taking every ounce of willpower I have not to rise from this chair, round the desk, stalk over to her, drag her into my arms, and pick up right where we left off on Friday night.

She presses her lips together in a thin line, her hands propped on her shapely hips. "I'm ordering lunch. What would you like?"

Her foot taps out a rhythm on the rug, the fire of her annoyance sending heat licking across my skin and straight to my crotch. I took for granted how even-tempered and professional Blaire always was before I asked her to help me find a wife and plan a wedding. She never let her emotions or her personal feelings about something cloud her ability to do her job well. But now, that line between professional and personal has been crossed, and it seems it's broken the dam on her self-restraint.

I clear my throat and shift uncomfortably. "I won't need anything today. I'm having lunch with Jessica."

Her foot stops. She shifts her stance. Her jaw clenches and shoulders tighten. "Alrighty, then."

She turns and mumbles something I can't quite make out.

Something about the chosen one?

CHAPTER 14

BLAIRE

I slam my fingers against my keyboard. Instead of helping me release some of my anger, the rhythmic clicks of the keys only seem to ratchet my aggression up even higher.

Who the hell does Archie think he is?

He spent all day yesterday and all morning today ordering me around, asking me to do menial tasks.

He never has three coffees in the morning, let alone two mornings in a row. He doesn't need to review all the files he had me grab over the last day and a half. I *know* he doesn't because the only two things he's been working on are the Ferguson acquisition and trying to smooth-talk widow Lancaster into meeting with him now that she controls her late husband's company.

The man has teams of people working on anything else that needs to happen. And God knows he's not spending his time wedding planning since I secured the venue—with a little help from Archie's pocketbook to pay off the couple who were already planning to have their wedding there New Year's Eve—and everything else.

He's infuriating. He's annoying.

And he still hasn't even mentioned our kiss.

Was the experience so meaningless? Am I such a bad kisser? Was it so awful or trivial that I don't even warrant an honorable mention?

I slam my hands on the keyboard and let out a frustrated groan. Now that I followed his lead by never bringing up the kiss, I've allowed this charade to go on as a mostly unwilling participant. I should have said something. Should have confronted him about it the moment he walked in yesterday.

Stupid Grinches. Stupid mistletoe.

I stop finger-punching my keyboard to take a drink of water and stretch my arms. The elevator dings, and I steel myself for what's about to come. The doors slide open, and the source of all my annoyance and frustration saunters out casually.

Despite my anger, I can't help but let my eyes roam over him. His ruffled dark hair suggests the stress of the day has forced him to rake his hand over his head several times. The deep-set blue eyes I stared into Friday night before his lips met mine look tired beneath inky brows. And the hard planes of muscle beneath his suit that bunch and flex as he moves make my stupid fingers twitch to trace their shape again.

Archie is the epitome of what a man should be. On the surface, at least. Beneath that posh, confident exterior lies a steaming pile of confusion. He's willing to give up his own happiness to secure control of this company.

How messed up is that?

His long strides bring him to my desk in a matter of seconds, which doesn't give me nearly enough time to prepare myself. "Blaire, any messages?"

Gee, nice greeting.

"Nope." I pop the *P*, my annoyance with him evident in every single thing I do or say.

Yet, despite that, I stare up at him, and for a moment, I get lost in what if.

What if he didn't have this marriage hanging over his head?

What if this company wasn't all that he wanted?

What if our kiss could have been the start of something magical?

My stupid Christmas-filled heart still holds out hope for him, even though the logical, real-world me knows it's useless.

His head tilts, and he twists his lips into a stern frown as he considers me. "Blaire, step into my office, please."

He heads toward his office, expecting me to follow and pauses outside the door.

Crap. I'm probably about to get written up or fired for my insubordination.

Great.

I huff out an annoyed sigh before pushing my chair away from my desk to stand. Apparently, I haven't just been rough on the keyboard today because my dress is a wrinkled mess. I run a hand down the shiny green fabric and make my way to his office. He stands, holding open the door, and as I pass, I chance a look at him. Archie's eyes flare with something that I can't understand.

Annoyance most likely.

He follows me in, removing his jacket before he walks behind his desk and drapes it over the back of his chair. "You've been short with me all week, Blaire. Is there something wrong? Have I done something to upset you?"

I inhale a deep breath and rub two fingers between my brows.

Surely, this intelligent man isn't so thick-headed.

"Are you serious right now?" It isn't really a question, more of a statement of incredulous anger. "You're joking? Please, tell me you're joking. You truly have no idea why I might possibly be upset with you? None?"

He pulls out his chair, takes a seat, and repositions himself somewhat nervously, squaring his shoulders. "I think it has to do with our kiss, but I'm not sure why there's all of this...hostility."

He gestures with a hand at the space between us, as if to encompass *us,* and it takes every ounce of control I have not to rail on him.

"Archie. You *kissed* me, and not just some friendly little peck under the mistletoe."

No, not some little kiss at all. He made my toes curl in my damn boots.

I'm fairly positive had we not been in a public setting that far more than a kiss would have transpired.

I mimic his motion between us. "Then...nothing. You've pretended like it didn't happen since the moment our lips parted. I saw the look on your face. You regretted it instantly."

I cross my arms over my chest as if that puts up some impenetrable shield around my heart. The truth is that the lack of acknowledgment on his part regarding our kiss has left me second-guessing myself endlessly.

Was I the only one who felt that jolt between us?

He nods slowly like he's considering my words and is just now realizing where the issue might lie. "I see. Well, I'm sorry this has troubled you. I just thought it was better for all involved to sweep it under the rug, so to speak."

"Sweep it under the rug? You're serious?"

My frustration builds, tightening my skin. I now see the truth. He didn't mention it because it didn't matter.

I don't matter.

In his world, apparently, a little kiss with your secretary isn't anything to get worked up about. But in mine, in *my* world, that kiss meant something. And that makes me the maddest of all.

My stupid hopeful heart. It's Christmas; it just seems like anything should be possible.

But this is what I get for being a romantic—hurt and embarrassed.

Too many romance novels and Christmas movies have me hopeful. When, really, all I am is a fool.

"Blaire, you misunderstand…"

"Stop." I hold up a hand to halt any further conversation. I'm through with this. It's hopeless, and Archie is unwilling to see the person right in front of him as anything more than an employee. "You're a moron."

And so am I for even hoping there could actually be anything of substance between us. I beeline for my desk, yank the drawer open, and grab my things because I'm over this day. I'm over this week, and right now, I'm over his dumb handsome face.

His office door swings open, and Archie storms out. "Blaire, wait a minute, please."

I turn to face him as I shoulder my bag. "I'm going home for the day. Call it a sick day if you want."

I'm sick, all right. Sick of his obliviousness and arrogance.

ARCHIMEDES

I stand dumbfounded beside Blaire's desk as the elevator doors close behind her.

What in the hell just happened?

When we kissed, I knew it was something—different,

wonderous, and not nearly enough—but the way she acted afterward, I assumed she regretted it instantly.

And why wouldn't she?

I'm her boss and about to get married to another woman. Of course, it'd be awkward for her. It's awkward for me. Carrying on as if it never happened seemed best for both of us.

But apparently, I misjudged her.

And that hurts like a bitch.

I can deal with my parents' disappointment. Hell, sometimes I even relish it from them, but not from Blaire. That's a look I'd never want to see on her face, let alone be the cause of putting it there. It's one of the reasons I dug that ugly sweater out of the trash and went to that party in the first place.

Shit. Now what do I do?

Call her? Go after her? Leave her alone?

No answer seems to be the right one.

My cell phone rings, and a tiny bead of hope lights in my chest that it might be Blaire. I pull it out of my pocket and sigh.

"Hey, Art."

His laugh tumbles through the line. "Wow, that good a day, little brother?"

"Yeah, just great." I rub the back of my neck and move back to my office.

I definitely don't need to stand out in the open and air my dirty laundry.

"How's your bride to be?"

"She's...well, not exactly my bride to be officially yet."

"I thought you were proposing this past weekend?"

"Uh, yeah. Actually, there's something I could use your advice about. Do you have a minute?" I lower myself into my desk chair.

A door shuts somewhere behind Artie. "I always have a minute for you, brother. What's going on?"

I steel my nerves.

What the hell will Artie say when I come clean?

"I went to a party last Friday, and at the party...I kissed Blaire underneath some mistletoe."

He chuckles. "Okay. It's tradition, so I don't think that's a huge deal. A little peck, although unprofessional, isn't that bad..."

"I kissed the hell out of her, Art, then went back in for seconds. God help me, I want to do it again and again. I cannot stop thinking about this woman."

The wrong woman.

"Oh. Oh, shit. Well, that is problematic, isn't it?"

I lean my head into the palm of my hand. "Yeah, just slightly. What do I do?"

"What does Blaire have to say about it?"

"My guess? Probably a lot more than she actually *did* say. She just tore into me because I didn't address it then or at all this week. I thought that's what she wanted. You know? I thought that's the way she wanted it handled until she told me off and left work early right before you called. She just stormed out. It's a mess."

I'm a mess.

It's becoming readily apparent that I handled this the wrong way. Though, I have no idea what the *right* way might be.

I stand and pace the length of my office, my free hand clenching into a fist and opening at my side.

Artie releases a concerned sound. "So, you like her?"

No. Yes. Maybe?

I groan into the phone like a love-sick fool. "Dammit, I do like her. What the hell am I supposed to do? I can't act on it.

Nothing can happen. It can't go anywhere. I'm days away from marriage."

"Yes, a loveless marriage. Archie, I need you to listen to me. Really listen. There are far more important things in this world besides our name and that company. Take it from someone who knows. Choosing myself, choosing Pen and Max, was the best decision that I have ever made. Really, there wasn't even a choice."

"We aren't in the same situation, Art. You had a family that needed you. You had options that I don't have."

I've always worked for Warren Enterprises. This life is the only one I know. Artie had his law degree and the ability to use that any way he wanted. I have my business degree and a talent for corporate takeovers.

Where is that going to get me?

Artie sighs his frustration down the line. "Archie, don't overlook the one thing, the one person, who could make you happiest. You should at least talk with Blaire. See where she stands. You never know what could be if you don't try."

His words offer no comfort. Only more confusion. "Okay, Art. Thanks. I'm going to go. I need to figure this out. I'll talk to you later."

"Archie, you already know what you need to do."

The line goes dead, and I toss my phone onto my desk so I can scrub my hands down my face.

He makes it sound so easy. It's not. He never gave a shit about Warren Enterprises. Not like me. It was always his to have by birthright. He never knew what it felt like to want this company with everything you have and know it would never happen. But now that I'm so close, I can't let it go.

Artie is right about one thing, though. I do need to talk to Blaire. She's the one real thing in my day-to-day life. That is definitely worth protecting, even if it's never anything but her being the best damn assistant in the world.

CHAPTER 15

BLAIRE

I can't believe I just stormed out of work like that, but I couldn't stay there one more second. Archie's refusal to even acknowledge something happened under the mistletoe was the last straw on an already hectic workday.

If I had stayed, I would have said or done something I would have regretted. Something that would have cost me a job I very much need.

I pull the cork from my favorite bottle of red wine and pour myself a hefty glass.

This day calls for it.

Wine in hand, I head toward my favorite chair in the living room, right next to the glittering Christmas tree. I set down my glass before I plop onto the comfy cushions and drag out my e-reader.

There's nothing like getting lost in a good romance novel after a long, difficult day. Unlike the real world, the characters are guaranteed a happily ever after, and the men always come around instead of acting like arrogant assholes.

The knock at the door interrupts the first line I try to read.

Who in the world could that be?

I throw off the blanket from my lap, drop the e-reader onto the couch, and make my way toward the door. I'm not expecting anyone, and with all the creeps and weirdos in New York City, it pays to be cautious. I lift up onto my tiptoes to look through the peephole. My heart stops, and my breath catches.

Archie? What's he doing here?

Maybe he came to fire me. I wouldn't be surprised.

I glance down at myself. Archie has never seen me in anything but work attire, but I'm not taking the time to change out of my leggings, tank top, and cardigan just to look *appropriate* for my boss, who I'm probably just going to argue with anyway.

It's best to just get this over with. Like ripping off a Band-Aid. I swing open the door with a scowl. My RBF is solid. "What are you doing here? Was there something I needed to do before I left work?"

He leans casually against the door jamb, his hands tucked into his pockets, and if I didn't want to throttle him so much, I might find him extremely attractive right now.

"Blaire, can we talk?"

I prop my hands on my hips. "I thought we already did that. What could you possibly have to say, Archie?"

He sighs deeply while looking down at his shoes like the answers lie there at his feet. When he raises his eyes to meet mine again, the blue there has softened. "That I'm sorry."

"Sorry for what, exactly?"

Ignoring my feelings? Making me feel like I didn't matter? Or one of the other myriad reasons I'm so pissed off at him right now?

His gaze travels from my face down to my breasts. I peek down to see my nipples hard and pointing straight at him.

Damn, not wearing a bra.

I pull my cardigan tighter around myself.

His chuckle rumble runs through me, teasing me, taunting me with the same seduction he worked on me Friday night.

Hell no. Not this time, mister.

He's not going to charm his way out of this.

He raises his eyebrows and motions behind me. "Can I come in, Blaire?"

I should say no. I should slam the door in his face, but he *is* my boss, and if I want to continue working at Warren Enterprises, we need to figure out a way to play nice. With a sigh, I step back from the door and motion him into my space.

He shoves off the jamb and walks past, his scent wafting straight over me.

So help me, God.

I take a deep inhale, and every nerve ending flares in response.

I hate being so weak where he is concerned, but he smells too damn good.

Archie takes a seat on my couch as if he's entitled. "First, I want to say thank you for letting me come in. Thank you for giving me an opportunity to speak with you. I'm sorry if not discussing what happened between us on Friday caused you any stress."

I hate to admit he looks good sitting on my couch—like he belongs there.

Damn him.

It's like I can't even stay mad at him. One disarming look is all it takes.

I clear my throat and cross my arms over my chest. "I appreciate your apology. But I believe this could've waited until tomorrow. It's not like that kiss meant anything."

To him, that is; and I was a fool for thinking otherwise.

"You're wrong, Blaire." He leans forward and rests his elbows on his knees. "It did mean something to me. It meant a lot to me. It actually meant more than I was willing to recognize at the time."

Huh. Well, I certainly didn't expect that admission.

"In fact," he rubs the back of his neck and sighs, "it's all I've been able to think about since the moment my lips touched yours. All I wanted to do was kiss you a hundred times a day, every day, all day."

What?

"Archie, is this some kind of joke?

It's not funny if it is. I've already settled what transpired between us. I don't want to process another round.

"Blaire, it is definitely not a joke." He stands and slowly stalks toward me.

The air in the room suddenly feels thicker, like it's harder to draw into my lungs.

Archie stops in front of me and holds his hands out. "If things could be different, if things *were* different, I would have taken you home with me that night." He reaches out and brushes my hand with his, then pulls it free to entwine our fingers. "Because that's what I really wanted to do. I would have my way with you every day at work." He flashes a roguish smile that sends chills over my skin. "I would have had you in my bed every available moment. And I would've made love to you every spare second of every single day since that kiss last Friday."

I crane my neck back to look him in the eyes but can't manage to form any words in response.

He brushes his free hand across my cheek. "You just don't get it, do you, Blaire? That kiss with you meant more than I could ever hope to imagine. And if it's okay with you, I'd like to do it again. Right now. So, tell me, Blaire, do you want me to kiss you?"

Holy shit.

"Y-y-yes," I manage to stammer out the word on a relieved sigh, and a second later, his mouth is on mine.

Claiming me.

Dominating me.

Consuming me.

This kiss is a thousand times better than the one we shared last Friday—because other than sheer desire, there's no reason for it. There's no mistletoe overhead tonight. No group of people egging us on. No Grinches interfering with our senses.

There's just...us.

His fingers glide into the hair at the nape of my neck, and he shifts my head, moving me just where he wants me... and where I want to be.

"Blaire," he whispers against my lips. "I'm sorry."

"Don't worry about it." I press my mouth back against his. *God, can you shut up already? Just kiss me.*

His hands leave my hair to slowly glide down my back to cup my ass. He groans and pushes his hardness against me, and I can't help but moan my appreciation into his mouth.

"Fuck, Blair. Fuck."

He lifts me easily, and I wrap both my legs around his waist, pinning his hard-on right where I want it the most.

"Bedroom. Bedroom." I chant between kisses. "Down the hall to the right."

I can't even worry about why I'm doing this or what will happen tonight or tomorrow.

All that matters is right here, right now, in this moment with Archie. When I'm in his arms, everything seems right.

❄

ARCHIMEDES

Has anything ever felt so right?

If so, I can't remember it. My heart thunders against my ribcage carrying Blaire toward her bedroom. Her kisses make me lightheaded, drunk, euphoric. As far as I'm concerned, I could now die a happy man with Blaire in my arms.

"Bedroom, bedroom, bedroom," she chants again.

I admire her enthusiasm and agree wholeheartedly; I can't get us there fast enough. Slowing down would only give me—us—time to think about what we're doing and all the reasons not to.

Right now, I don't want to think about anything but being inside her and seeing what she looks like when she comes.

I kick her bedroom door open with my foot, unwilling to take my hands off her magnificent ass. I can't wait to get her out of these clothes, unwrap her and finally see all of her.

Because Blaire Hall is about to give me the best gift of the season.

My lips never leave hers as I take us to the bed, turn, and set her on my lap. I don't want to waste a second with her.

Finally, after a year of looking at her sexy ass in tight skirts, festive Christmas sweaters that cling to her tits, and her mile-long legs, I get to see what lies underneath. My usually steady hands shake, pushing the cardigan off her shoulders. I yank the tank top off over her head and pull her hair from the bun at the back. A cascade of silky red strands falls across her shoulders.

Her bare shoulders.

Shit. She doesn't have on a bra.

My focus dips to her exposed breasts, and I suck in a deep breath. "Good Lord, Blaire. You're phenomenal."

I can't resist her exposed flesh and reach out to grab her

left breast while my left hand and mouth go in the opposite direction.

She dips her head back and moans. "Oh, Archie."

I know, sweetheart. I know. I'm right there with you.

She pushes at my jacket and manages to get it halfway down my arms before she moves to try to unbutton my shirt. But it's taking far too long. I pop us up off the bed and set her onto her feet.

I can't wait any longer to get her naked.

"Let's get these clothes off."

She sheds her leggings in no time, and I'm right behind her, my hands flying over buttons and zippers to get naked as soon as possible. I keep one eye on her as she pushes her panties to the floor and practically jumps out of them.

I guess she's as anxious as I am to get things started.

A deep chuckle rumbles from my chest, and I retrieve my wallet from my pants, pull out a condom, and lay it on the nightstand. "Get on the bed, Blaire, on your back."

She does as instructed, sprawling out across the mattress, her soft, pale skin glowing in the light of the moon shining in from the window to our left and her auburn hair spilling like a halo around her head on the pillow. I stroke myself and watch her breasts rise and fall with her sharp inhalations. She watches me slide my hand along my shaft, and her green eyes darken.

Fuck, she's more than a bastard like me deserves, but I'll be damned if I don't enjoy her every curve.

I've wanted her and this moment for a long time. I just never let myself believe it was possible.

The fiery crown of her hair calls out to me, making my fingers inch to run through it, and I make my way toward her, grab her foot, and pull her to the edge of the bed.

I drop to my knees and lift her ankle to my lips. She yelps

in surprise then groans as I kiss my way up her leg to that beautiful spot right at the apex of her thighs.

My mouth descends on her pussy. Blaire thrashes against the sheets, and her hands push into my hair. She pulls on it, shifting my head and showing me just where she needs me. Like the gentleman I am, I oblige, thrusting my tongue inside her then up around her clit.

"Shit. Shit. Right there, Archie." She practically purrs my name.

The sound only spurs me on, and with a few more flicks of my tongue, she detonates, bucking against me and coming against my mouth.

And I relish every last drop of her pleasure.

Seeing her come undone, knowing I am the one who did it makes my cock throb, and I stroke it and slowly kiss my way up her torso, admiring her flawless skin. I reach over to grab the condom, but she grabs my wrist.

"Let me do it." She smiles devilishly, takes the condom from my hand, and tears it open.

I've never let a woman do this before. It somehow seems more personal, more intimate.

She begins to roll it down my shaft, and I have to bite my lip to keep from letting out a slew of curse words that sit on the tip of my tongue. Her touch is maddening, and if she lingers with her hands on me any longer, I may lose the battle with my willpower and end things embarrassingly fast.

Thank God...

With the condom fully on, I can finally take a deep breath, but then she slides her hands up and down my cock a few times, and I've had all the foreplay that I can take.

I lean over her and press my body against hers until she lies flat on her back. "You're gorgeous, Blaire."

An absolute vision. Her bright-red lips, already swollen

from our kissing, beg for my mouth, and I drop my head and kiss her while I align myself with her wet core.

I push into her tight heat slowly, savoring the feel of her clasping around me.

Christ.

This is Heaven and I've been living in a Hell of my own making by fighting this for so long.

Pulling my mouth from hers, I search her face. "Are you okay?"

She clenches me inside her in response and rolls her hips, shifting me even deeper. "Yes, perfect."

She *is* perfect. Sexy, smart, beautiful, fun, unexpected, and a breath of fucking fresh air in my stale life.

Her legs come up and wrap around me, shifting my position slightly and eliciting a groan from deep in my chest.

I pull out and plunge back inside her. Tension coils in my body, wanting to drive hard and fast, but I muster every ounce of restraint to hold myself back. Because...I need this to last. This feeling of being wrapped up with her, moving together as one.

Her hips meet mine—every thrust bringing me back home and every withdrawal just a momentary separation of what feels so damn right.

I angle my hips back, changing our positions just enough that the head of my cock drags against her G-spot. Her eyes roll back, and her mouth falls open. I capture her gasps of pleasure with a deep, demanding kiss as I drive us closer to the precipice of ecstasy.

"Look at me, Blaire."

The only thing that could make this moment more perfect would be her gaze locked on mine when we both fall over that edge.

She follows my command and tilts her head until our

eyes lock again. Pure desire stares back at me—a desperate need that matches my own.

I push into her, my rhythm faltering slightly as a slow burn starts at the base of my spine. I grit my teeth.

Looking into her eyes, kissing her soft lips, feeling her flesh pressed against mine, I fall further and further into trouble where my heart is concerned.

Blaire Hall is the most amazing woman I've ever met.

But all of this is just a fantasy.

As good as this feels right now. As *right* as it feels…

It will be gone tomorrow when reality slaps me in the face.

Blaire's nails dig into my shoulders, and she gasps as her orgasm slams into her. I sink into her one final time, burying myself as deep as possible and release everything I've been holding inside—the anguish, the fear, the longing, and the feelings I have for this woman I can't dare even think about.

CHAPTER 16

BLAIRE

We have the cake tasting at eleven-thirty, right?

I stare down at the text message from Archie.

Seriously?

So, we banged last night, and now we're just going to head to the cake tasting like nothing happened?

My fingers hover over my phone, and it is so tempting to write that very thing to him.

It was weird enough waking up after incredible sex to find him—and all signs of him save for the used condoms in the trash can—gone without a word. Then I had to come into the office, not knowing what to say.

But his last-minute meeting with the widow Lancaster saved me from that awkward moment—at least for a little while. I haven't had to see him yet, haven't had to look into the same eyes that locked with mine while he made love to me and wonder what the hell we're going to do now.

Apparently, if this text is any sign, we're going to pretend nothing happened and move along with the wedding plans.

Nothing like helping the boss who just had his mouth on every inch of your body pick out some wedding cake.

Yes. See you there.

I guess my boss booty-called me last night.

I shouldn't be surprised, though, should I?

He's been stringing me along like lights on a Christmas tree since our first kiss. His hot one minute, cold the next attitude is giving me whiplash.

It's not that I expected an undying declaration of love, but I would think that last night might mean *something*. Perhaps give him *some* pause about marrying someone else next week.

I guess I was wrong.

Again.

I grab my bag from my desk, stalk over to the elevator, and jab the down button a little too forcefully. If I don't get a handle on my frustration before I go into that bakery, it's going to make things even more uncomfortable. Poor Anne Marie thought she was winning the lottery by being selected to handle the cake for such a high-profile wedding.

The poor woman has no idea what a shit-show this all is.

The fresh, cold air on the short two-block walk to the bakery does me some good. There's a lot to be said for a few good deep, cleansing breaths, and I almost feel like I'm in control by the time I open the door and the smell of sugar and spices hit my nose.

A little moan slips out.

It smells like heaven in here.

I scan the small space and scowl. Archie sits perched atop a black iron cafe chair, his large form nearly concealed by the confections stacked up before him.

He rises and offers me a typical Warren smile. "Blaire, you made it."

Don't be fooled by that sparkle in his eye, Blaire. It's a lie.

He's excited his wedding planner with perks is here.

A short blonde with a contagious smile rises from the chair across from him and extends her hand. "Hello. I'm Anne Marie. You must be Blaire."

We shake while Archie pulls out the chair beside him for me.

"Blaire Hall. It's lovely to finally meet you."

Anne Marie waves a hand toward the table. "Let's start, shall we? I've made samples of all the flavors you've requested, Blaire. Which do you want to start with?"

I survey the parchment-lined silver tray. Beautifully decorated tiny cakes lay before me, with their names written out on cards in front of each one.

Immediately, I find my favorite. My dream winter wedding cake straight from my notebook brought to life— just like I requested when I spoke with Anne Marie the other day. I can almost forget Archie and his insulting treatment, knowing I'm about to have this cake. "Anne Marie, is this it?"

She smiles as I gently grab the cake and pull it toward me.

"It is, and it is actually my favorite. Honestly, I would have never thought of this combination, but it makes so much sense together." She slices off a piece of the cake and sets it on my dessert plate.

Gingerbread and eggnog creme.

It smells like the holidays and every good memory that I have ever had, including every daydream of my future wedding plans. This concoction has been in my mind and my notebook for years. And she managed to pull it off.

Archie leans in to check out the cake. "That sounds good, actually. Smells even better."

I cast him a side-eye. I don't care what he thinks. He can serve himself. I pick up my fork and slice off a bite.

This cake is for me. A totally selfish indulgence.

And after the way he has been treating me, I've earned it.

I lift my dream cake to my lips, and the spicy confection hits my taste buds. A deep moan floats out around my fork.

Archie coughs and clears his throat, shifting in his seat and looking more flustered than I've ever seen him. "That must be some good cake."

He releases an awkward chuckle and watches me, like he's trying to decide how he should be handling the situation.

I continue to ignore him, because — cake.

If he can pretend things are fine, so can I.

Anne Marie places a piece in front of him. "Here, Mister Warren. Try it. I think your bride-to-be is sold. You two make a lovely couple, by the way. I've been in this business long enough to know a happily in love couple when I see it, and you two are it. "

Poor Anne Marie. Poor, delusional Anne Marie.

She has no idea the handsome man before her is a total asshole.

It's okay, Anne Marie. He fooled me, too.

Archie's eyes widen, and he shifts uncomfortably again, rubbing the back of his neck and averting his gaze from mine. "Blaire? Oh, no. Uh...you're mistaken, Anne Marie. I'm...not marrying Blaire. She's just my assistant."

Just. My. Assistant.

His words hit me like heavy-weight punches.

And they're the last straw.

I swallow the bite in my mouth and force a saccharine-sweet smile. "No, we are definitely not getting married."

A mirthless laugh bubbles from my lips, although nothing about this situation is funny.

The delicious cake I've waited my entire life for suddenly doesn't seem so perfect, but I take a final bite anyway before standing.

Archie looks at me with his brow twisted. He starts to get up, like he wants to say something or is going to try to stop me, but he lowers himself back down again, his hands clenched at his sides.

He looks confused, something that I no longer am.

I'm finished with him. Finished with this tasting.

Even though I'd love to leave him hanging, I'll finish the rest of the wedding planning, because I agreed to. And unlike him, I see my commitments through. Fortunately, the office will be closed for the holidays starting this afternoon, so I won't have to see this asshole until the day of the wedding. But before I go, there's something he needs to hear. I'm just sorry Anne Marie has to be around for it. Poor woman.

I zone in on a still-shocked Archie and shake my head. "I'm sorry you were confused, Anne Marie. Archie and I aren't a couple. We aren't anything. I'm only good enough to get his coffee, fetch his files, and plan his wedding."

His eyes widen, and he holds up a hand. "Blaire, please stop. Let's discuss—"

I cut him off. I'm not listening to him again. "There's nothing to discuss. You've made it clear. I'm good enough to do all those things, but I'm not good enough to treat with respect, right?"

That hurts the most. He could have stayed. We could have talked about what happened. We could have figured it out. Instead, he's just moving forward with this sham like we didn't share *that* last night.

"Blaire, please calm down." He shifts forward on his chair toward me. "This is not the time or the place for this. Can we discuss this elsewhere?"

Archie apparently hasn't learned—as most men haven't—that telling a woman to calm down is going to have the opposite effect.

My face must say it all. He holds up his hands in surrender or to protect himself, with his eyes wide and scared—like he's about to get in a cage and try to rein in a raging lioness.

But it's too late, too much has happened, too much has been done.

"Calm down?" I shake my head in disgust.

This is about as calm as it's going to get for me. He has used me at every turn to plan for this wedding. All I wanted was for him to be happy. To have the perfect day. It's why I gave him my wedding, the one I've been planning since I was a child. And he doesn't appreciate any of it. Or me.

My hands shake, and tears burn the back of my eyes, but I'm not going to cry in front of him. Oh, no. I'm not going to give him the satisfaction.

"I hope you and your bride are happy, and I hope you enjoy my wedding cake." I reach for the rest of the piece on my plate, pick it up with my hand, and smash it into Archie's face. The soft cake and frosting smear across his skin easily.

And it feels fantastic.

I fling the excess cake onto his crotch and wipe my hand off on the shoulder of his Armani suit.

"Oh, my." Anne Marie jumps to her feet.

Archie just sits there stunned as the crumbs tumble down his chest and into his lap. He opens and closes his mouth, trying to find something to say, but apparently, I've rendered him speechless.

I grab my bag and turn to Anne Marie. "Thank you for your time. That cake was amazing, and I'm sorry about the mess. Just bill him. He's good for it."

Without another word, I head toward the door and pull it open. The cool air engulfs me, but it can't stop the tears. As soon as I round the corner, the dam opens, and they flow like a river.

Because no matter how hurt and angry I may be at Archie, I'm even more devastated with how things have ended.

With my heart as smashed as the cake on his face.

ARCHIMEDES

I watch Blaire walk away from the table and most likely out of my life, completely helpless to stop her. There aren't any words that can make what happened last night right, nothing that can stop her from fleeing from me—rightfully so.

What could I possibly do to salvage this clusterfuck?

She flings open the door to the bakery, sending the bells on the door chiming. The lonely sound echoes around the room. She doesn't even look back.

Final.

It feels final, and I suppose it is.

I'd like to say that I didn't deserve what just happened, but I did, likely far worse.

When I woke up last night with Blaire sated and wrapped in my arms, it felt right.

Too right.

I lay there in her bed, twirling her red curls around my finger, wishing things could be different. That I could be different. That my life could be different.

And I knew I wouldn't be able to look her in the eye when she woke up.

I wouldn't be able to stand that expression on her face—disappointment and disgust. I would have to leave her there, leave us there, in the sanctuary of her bed, because she's a possibility I want but that can never be.

It turns out, I was right.

The way she just looked at me shattered my heart into a million pieces.

I'm a selfish bastard, and I wanted her. I wanted something to cling to, one moment in time where she could be mine, just a piece of her, however small it might be. That's all

153

that can ever exist of Blaire and me, and I will guard it, cherish it for the rest of my miserable life.

So, instead of facing her last night, I left, like the coward I am. Somehow thinking, if we just pushed on with the wedding plans, she would understand what happened and why.

That it was me saying goodbye to her.

I thought she would know what last night was without me explaining it in excruciating detail.

What more could I say that would make any of this easier for her? Nothing.

In the end, though, nothing I can say or do matters.

This fucked-up situation is my reality, and now, she's in the middle of it with me.

That special and amazing woman is everything I want. But I can't force this life on her. My reality is harsh and often cruel, and Blaire is everything wonderful. I couldn't stand to see my world tarnish her.

This fucking wedding will be the death of me.

I hope the Warrens are happy that this is what my life has become.

"Oh, Mister Warren, oh my goodness. Let me go get you something to clean up with. I'm so sorry. I didn't mean to cause an issue, you just," Anne Marie waves her hands in the air between us, "you two just seem so right together."

I feel the same way, Anne Marie.

We just...work. Professionally and personally, things just click when Blaire and I are together. We so easily fall into that rhythm, the one that would make a future together so natural. But there's nothing natural about the situation or life I find myself in. Not when I have no control over what's going to happen in the next week. That control was taken from me the moment Grandfather signed that revised trust.

Anne Marie holds out a linen napkin to me. "Every time I

talked to her on the phone, she kept telling me how this was her dream cake. I'm sorry, I just assumed that you were the bride and groom."

"It's okay, Anne Marie. It's an honest mistake." I grab the napkin, lick my lips, and wipe my face.

It's damn good cake, and this is actually the one thing about this God-forsaken wedding planning that I was looking forward to. Just like everything else with this farce of a wedding, it's ruined.

I'm not a superstitious man, but I am beginning to wonder if this wedding isn't cursed. It's ruining my life in more ways than I even anticipated.

Anne Marie hustles off like her ass is on fire. She can't get away fast enough, and I can't blame her or Blaire. I'd get as far away from me as possible if I were them.

I am an asshole, and I deserve everything that just happened and then some.

This is the end for Blaire and me on a personal and professional level. I'll have to send her a thank you gift of some sort for all that she has done to plan this wedding.

Though, she may not be willing to accept it, so maybe a bonus would be better. Something I can put straight into her account. And I'll have to transfer her to work for someone else in the company, if she's even willing to *work* in the same building as me anymore.

Shit.

I don't even care about work.

Is our friendship salvageable at this point?

I doubt it.

Definitely not after I left her alone in bed this morning. I don't think there's any coming back from that. That's the part that slices away at my heart the most. I didn't just lose someone I'm attracted to; at this point, I've lost my friend. We've grown so close over the last few weeks, and honestly,

I'm not sure what my life would be like without her in it. Other than empty.

Blaire has really stepped up to the plate to help me through all this mess. She single-handedly took it all on, in stride, and managed to pull this entire clusterfuck together. I wouldn't be about to secure this company, my dream, without her.

She's an amazing fucking woman, and I screwed her over, literally.

"I brought you something to wipe off with. You can head on over to the restroom, and I'll get this mess cleaned up." Anne Marie places the towels down on the table and makes herself busy as I stand, cake falling to the floor.

"I'm sorry about the mess. I'll pay for your time and please, let me help you clean this up."

"She waves her hand at me. "Nonsense. Go on and get cleaned up. The restroom is down the hall." She points to her left.

"Thanks." I walk around the table and make my way toward the restroom with a guilty conscience and a heavy heart.

This is supposed to be the season of miracles. Frankly, I never bought into that theory, but I wouldn't turn one down right about now.

CHAPTER 17

BLAIRE

Before I started working for Warren Enterprises, I heard about how amazing the Warren Christmas party always was, and then, when I finally experienced it for myself, I understood why everyone loved it so much.

One thing the Warrens know how to do is throw a party. And the Christmas Eve bash is always the biggest. The one where they pull out all the stops and probably spend more money than I've made in my entire life on one night. And this year is no exception. They even rented out The American Museum of Natural History rather than hosting it at their estate.

Normally, I'd be thrilled to be here. The decorations. The drinks and the food. The beautiful people decked out to the nines to impress everyone else. It really is a sight to behold and an experience.

But after what went down with Archie at the cake tasting yesterday, it's the last place I want to be.

Getting into my dress, putting on my makeup and a fake

smile, and forcing myself to come tonight was one of the hardest things I've ever had to do in my life...while smashing that cake in Archie's face seemed easy. It happened before I even thought about it or could stop myself. And even though it probably means I'll be looking for a new job after the new year, he deserved it, so I won't say I regret seeing it all over him.

If I weren't required to be here for my job, I would be anywhere else. Though, likely just sitting home alone on the couch watching Hallmark Christmas movies and crying some more.

What else can I do?

There's nothing I can say that's going to change Archie's mind.

He proved that the way he just walked into the room with a smile on the lips that kissed me only two days ago while he has another woman on his arm. It makes the champagne I just downed gurgle in my stomach and threaten to come up my throat.

How can he act like what happened between us meant nothing and just move on with this wedding with her?

The Chosen One looks up at him with puppy dog eyes from under long lashes, and he smiles at her and leans down to whisper something in her ear. My hand tightens around the stem of the glass, and I force myself to turn away from them and focus on the rest of the party. If I don't, I'm liable to say or do something stupid.

This is the very reason you never get romantically involved with a coworker, let alone your boss. Yet, I fell hook, line, and sinker for the Warren charm. Let myself be lulled into a false sense of security because I thought I knew the man, because I thought I understood what he needs and wants, but apparently, I was totally wrong.

I blink away the sting of tears and down the rest of the

champagne. A waiter walks by with a tray of full glasses, and I drop my empty and scoop up another full one.

"Whoa. Slow down there, tiger. The night is still young."

I freeze with the glass halfway to my lips and turn slowly toward the man who is the source of so much passion—good and bad.

Archie flashes me the trademark Warren grin despite the fact the last time we saw each other, I shoved cake in his face.

I glance behind him. "Where is The Chosen One? I'm surprised she lets you get ten feet away from her."

His smile falters, and he presses his lips into a hard, thin line. I turn to walk away from him, but his hand snaps out. He grabs my elbow tightly, and I glance down at where our bodies connect.

"What the hell are you doing, Archie?"

He leans into me, the smell of his leathery, rich cologne permeating the air and making my body heat at the memory of that scent all over me and in my bed. But instead of giving me an answer, he practically drags me around the corner and down a short hallway off the main party.

Now that we're totally alone, I finally jerk him off me and wheel to face him. "What the hell do you think you're doing?"

His lips twist into a scowl. "I could ask you the same thing. What was with that comment?"

I raise an eyebrow. "What comment?"

He snorts out a laugh. "The Chosen One?" One of his eyebrows wings up. "Is that really what you call her?"

Now it's my time to snort and take a sip of my champagne, which somehow miraculously didn't spill during his aggressive maneuver. "Isn't she, though? It sure as hell isn't me."

Shit.

I hadn't meant to say that part out loud. Downing that first glass so fast on an empty stomach wasn't such a good idea for my filter. Though, I haven't really had much of one around him since this entire wedding fiasco started.

The hardness in Archie's gaze dissipates, and he takes a step toward me. "Don't be like that, Blaire."

I scoff and shake my head. "Like what, Archie? Like it's the truth? Because it is. You've made it abundantly clear since Tuesday."

He winces and scrubs his hands over his face. "God, this is so fucked up."

That's a generous way of putting it. It's beyond "fucked up" to sleep with someone then go ahead with wedding plans to another woman the next day.

"Have you slept with her?" The question is out of my mouth before I can stop it.

He recoils slightly, his eyes wide. "Fuck, no. Of course, not…"

I raise my eyebrows. "Of course, not? She's your future wife. You're proposing tonight, aren't you?"

There's no need to further point out the lunacy in the situation. The flickering uncertainty in his blue eyes says it all. He holds up his hands, looking very much like a lost child instead of a billionaire CEO poised to have the entire Warren fortune at his fingertips permanently. "What is it you want me to do, Blaire?"

I swallow thickly, my mouth suddenly dry as a bone. "I…"

ARCHIMEDES

Her eyes shimmer with unshed tears, but she's on the verge of losing control.

I am, too.

My entire body vibrates, warring with itself between

taking her into my arms and kissing away her tears and turning back to the party and the woman I *have* to marry.

I haven't been able to stop thinking about her and what happened at the cake tasting. It's the *only* thing I've thought about. Instead of planning my proposal tonight to Jessica, I've been wracking my brain, trying to find a way to make things right with Blaire.

How messed up is that?

She swallows again and shifts her shoulders back in what I imagine is supposed to be a show of strength, but all it does is push her fantastic breasts out toward me and make my hands itch to touch them again.

I haven't been able to take my eyes off her since the second I walked into the party, and having Jessica on my arm felt like I was slapping Blaire in the face the way she basically did to me yesterday at the bakery.

And I can't say I blame her for doing it.

Planning a wedding for the man she just slept with isn't exactly high up on anyone's to-do list. Yet Blaire has been with me every step of the way. She's become my best friend, my confidante, the one I can trust through all this craziness. And all I've done is push her away and send her mixed signals.

Something I thought I was done with after yesterday.

I hadn't intended to approach her tonight. She needs space. And time.

And even with all that, she still may never forgive me or want to be in the same room with me ever again.

So, I wasn't going to talk to her. I certainly never planned on having this conversation at all, let alone here, of all places.

But like a moth drawn to the flame, as soon as Jessica left to use the bathroom, I floated toward Blaire, knowing it would hurt, knowing I would get burned. And now the pain tightening my chest is almost too much to bear.

If I feel this awful, I can't even imagine how she feels.

She struggles for her words, which only makes the pain over what I've done to her worse. Over the last few weeks, Blaire has never had a problem speaking her mind and telling me exactly how she feels. And now I've built this wall between us and created this tension that we'll never be able to overcome.

This means the end of our working relationship. We both know it. There's no way we can work together now and pretend like it's not breaking both of us. And it would be a lie to say it's not. Because I see it in her eyes; I see it in the way she holds herself, her protective stance like I'm going to hurt her and she's trying to ensure her own safety.

She takes a deep breath and swallows again, then straightens her shoulders and opens her beautiful, soft, pink lips. "I want you to choose me, Archie."

All the air suddenly feels like it's been sucked out of the hallway where we stand, and I struggle to take a breath.

I manage to swallow through the emotions clogging my throat. "You can't be serious."

One of the tears she's barely held back since almost the moment I walked in finally sneaks out of her right eye and trickles down her cheek through her immaculate makeup.

"I can't be serious?" She lets out a mirthless laugh and shakes her head again. "How can you stand there and pretend there's nothing going on between us? How can you stand there and pretend the other night didn't happen? *How?*"

Her words hit me like a ten-ton cannon, each one a blow to the carefully constructed future in a world I thought I had figured out in my head. The pain of each one builds on top of the others until my entire body might as well be on fire. The agony would probably be easier to bear than what she's doing to me right now. "Because I have to, Blaire."

I'd give anything to be able to take her into my arms and

kiss her and hold her there forever, but it's not reality. It's not the life I was ever meant to have. And it's not a life I would ever wish upon someone I care about so much.

But I can't ever say any of that to her.

Even though I want her to understand why things have to be this way, why I don't have any choice. I need her to know the last thing I ever want to do is hurt her, but the only words I can manage are, "I'm sorry."

I suck in a deep breath and rub the back of my neck. "I can't marry you, Blaire, even if I wanted to." I stop short of saying I do because admitting that would put her in exactly the position I'm trying to keep her from. Feeling obligated to enter into this freak show I call a family, people who would rather have me marry someone I barely know than be single. "Look at my family, Blaire…"

Father and Grandfather walking around in their tuxedoes with glasses of scotch worth more than the average person makes in a lifetime. Mother and Grandmother in jewelry and dresses fit for royalty. And all of it just a fucking act to impress people.

Her tears spill over and fall in earnest now, leaving little splashes on her red dress. "Yeah." She chokes back a sob and glances down at herself before meeting my gaze again. "And look at me."

CHAPTER 18

ARCHIMEDES

"Look at you?" I take another step closer to her, my hands fisted at my sides so hard, my nails bite into the skin. The sharp bite of pain helps keep me grounded in the present, a reminder of where we are and how we got here. If not for that, I might get lost in how scared and beautiful Blaire is and how badly I want to whisk her away from all this. "I *am* looking at you, Blaire. I've been looking at you, and I've seen you for years."

I shove a hand back through my hair and pace away from her. With that dress and her auburn curls flowing around her face, her perfect pouty lips quivering, I don't know that I can stop myself from doing something incredibly stupid.

How can she not understand?

Apparently, I did a very good job of concealing my attraction to her over the years because she honestly seems oblivious to it. And while it might be for the best to let her think I don't care, to let her believe I just wanted to get my dick wet before I got hitched, I can't stand the thought of her thinking that's all she's worth.

So instead, I force myself to meet her gaze, to stare into the same green eyes that I looked into while we made love only two nights ago, the ones I *want* to see every damn day of my life if things were simple.

"Christ, Blaire. You think I could miss you all this time? With your crazy dresses and your flashy shoes and your beautiful blazing-red hair? You think I haven't thought about what I would like to do to you for years prior to us ever hooking up?"

Her eyes widen with every word, and her bottom lip and the hand holding her drink tremble. She opens her mouth to say something, but almost immediately clamps it shut— either unsure what to say or unwilling to say it.

"Because I *have*, Blaire. Ever since you were an intern and we were both college students. That long ago. I *saw* you. And I've told myself over and over again that getting involved with one of my employees was really fucking bad news. It's the only thing that kept me from pursuing you sooner."

She slowly raises her glass to her lips with a shaking hand and downs it in one gulp.

I can't say I've ever seen Blaire so shaken before, and I can't really blame her for needing some liquid courage right now. I'd kill for a nice scotch. Or hell, even one of those Grinches.

Though the green concoction clearly did something to my head that prevented me from realizing what a mess I'd make by kissing her. If I'd never done that, I would never have opened this door. I could have kept the Blaire fantasy locked away forever.

Damn those Grinches!

I bet she could use one right now, too.

But the champagne seems to calm her momentarily, and

she narrows her eyes on me. "Then why are we even having this conversation?"

I release a heavy sigh, one full of regret and acceptance at the same time. "Because even if this *had* started sooner. Even if we had figured this out, it wouldn't have changed anything."

And that's the most painful part of all of this and the part she can't seem to grasp.

My life isn't my own. It hasn't been since the moment I was born a Warren.

"You're beautiful, Blaire, and fucking intelligent and funny and your own person unapologetically with a beautiful spirit that lights up a room…" I suck in a deep breath to steel myself for what I'm about to say because it's going to hurt both of us, but it's the damn truth, "and I would never ever subject you to the Warren family. They will kill everything good in you and crush that spirit. They'll turn you into an angry, bitter shell of a person, and that is the last thing I would ever wish for you."

Laughter from the party tinkles down the hallway, echoing joyfully around us when all I feel is utter despair right now. This party is always the highlight of the year for the family. One thing I've always excelled at is partying and presenting the perfect Warren façade. That's something I will never watch happen to Blaire—fake smiles around fake people.

Her inability to recognize that makes my heart pound in my chest, and no amount of deep breaths can calm it. Nor can it stop the word vomit pouring out of my mouth.

"You weren't made for this, Blaire, no matter how badly I may want you in my bed and my life. I would never do that to you. I *couldn't* do that to you. We can't always get what we want, Blaire. Sometimes…" I squeeze my eyes closed because saying these words to her while looking at her might break me completely, and there is an entire museum full of family and friends and socialites, any of whom could walk down the hallway at any moment and see me completely falling apart. "Sometimes, we have to settle."

BLAIRE

"Settle?" The word coming from his lips makes me wince, and the empty glass in my hand shakes violently beyond my control.

The man standing before me isn't the Archie I've come to know over the last few weeks. The man I'm looking at is Archimedes Leonidas Warren. This is the man who's been beaten down and whipped bloody and somehow convinced that the most important thing in his life is this damn company. This isn't the man I went to bed with, the man who was so laid-back and carefree at that party, even though he was completely out of his element. This is Archimedes, the businessman. This is Archimedes, the CEO.

"So, that's it?" I raise an eyebrow at him. "You're just going to give up on love so easily and marry that woman? The woman you barely know. The woman you've barely spent more than a handful of hours with? You're going to spend the rest of your life with her, have children with her, take her to family functions, and force a smile and pretend you're happy? Is the money really worth that to you?"

He growls low and takes a step toward me, anger flashing in his eyes. "You think this is about money?"

This man has a lot of nerve getting mad at me about this.

I press my lips together and harden my stance. "Isn't it?"

"Fucking hell, Blaire." He runs his hands through his already disheveled hair and glances behind him down the hallway toward the party where our disappearance has undoubtedly been noticed by now. "It's not about the money. It's about taking something my grandfather and father built, which has meant so much to my family and making it even better. This company is like their child, and it will be mine."

I snort and shake my head. "They care about it more than they care about any of their *actual* children, and you're falling right into the same trap."

He's going to live in a sham of a loveless marriage, have children with a woman he doesn't even care about, and all for a building and title.

"I'm not, Blaire, because I'm going in with my eyes open. I never thought I'd have this opportunity. We all assumed Artie would step up exactly as planned and slide right into the role when my father finally decides to formally retire. It was something I thought I could never have, and now, it's the only thing I can focus on."

My chest aches for the broken man in front of me. He's been so tainted by them, by this life, and by this world, that he's not even aware of his own insane tunnel vision.

"So, you're willing to give up on love for a company? I just want to make sure I'm clear on this."

He freezes, and his wide eyes search mine.

Shit.

The *L* world slipped from my lips before I could stop it. I certainly never intended to say it, and definitely not here tonight, not days before his wedding to another woman. Until he grabbed my arm and dragged me back here, I had accepted that I would have to watch that happen, but now, seeing how tormented he appears, I know there's a struggle there—between what he wants and what he thinks he can't have.

There's no reason he has to live like this. And now that

I've essentially told him I love him, I've offered him a way out. A way to me. He just has to take it.

He swallows thickly and reaches out to me but immediately pulls back his hand. Almost like he's forcing himself to stop when all he wants is exactly the same thing I do. For him to pull me into his arms, tell me he loves me, and that he's choosing me.

Instead, he takes two steps back, putting the physical distance between us that matches the emotional one I feel weighing on my shoulders. "Sometimes, love isn't enough, Blaire."

I should've expected it from him, but his words still hit me like a physical blow. The glass drops from my hand and shatters on the expensive marble tile.

Neither of us even glance down at it, our eyes locked on each other.

"That's really sad, Archie, that you really believe that, especially now," I wave a hand behind him toward the party, "during the Christmas season when miracles happen."

He heaves out a heavy sigh, one that matches the burden I see in him. "That's just it, Blaire. I've never believed in miracles."

With that final hit, he turns and walks away from me without a look back. Each step he takes echoes down to me, and Jessica appears at the end of the hallway and sees him. Her eyes light up, but when he reaches her, her smile falters. She glances down the hallway at me, concern etched on her sweet face. After a moment of examining me, she lifts her arm to his and guides him around the corner and out of view.

Archimedes Warren will never admit what Archie Warren and I have.

And I'm starting to believe miracles don't happen, either.

CHAPTER 19

ARCHIMEDES

Everything is so fucked up. And Jessica knows something is wrong. Despite my telling her that everything was fine and that Blaire was just upset about something work-related, I don't think she buys it.

How could she?

I can barely look her in the eye and can't stop my body from vibrating as we stand here chatting with...

Christ, who are we even talking to?

I scan the faces of the couple in front of us and force a smile. Senator Randall and his wife, Patsy. People I should be schmoozing instead of just standing here, staring at blankly. Jessica carries on the conversation from my side, the shyness I was initially concerned about apparently gone.

Thank God for that.

Right now, I'm utterly useless. I search the room. Thankfully, Father and Grandfather are on the far wall talking with the mayor. If either of them saw me like this, it would invite a lot of questions I don't have answers to.

"Excuse me?" The familiar voice behind me makes me let out a relieved breath. Athena rounds to my side and flashes a grin at everyone. "Can I borrow my brother for a minute?"

Jessica looks up at me, concern flickering in her gaze, but I offer her what I hope is a reassuring smile.

I lean in and press a kiss to her cheek. "I'll be right back."

Athena drags me across the main room, past dignitaries and co-workers, and out onto the balcony. Despite the space heaters out here, the cold, blustery, Christmas Eve air sends a shiver down my spine. In the shiny, strapless dress she's wearing, she must be freezing.

I shrug out of my jacket and hand it to her.

She flashes me a grin and shoves her arms into it. "Thanks."

"It's the least I can do for saving me back there."

"You looked like you were about ready to throw up. What's going on? I saw you disappear with Blaire, and when you came back, it looked like the rug had been ripped out from under you."

I rub my hands over my arms and stomp my feet to keep warm and avoid answering the question. If I tell Athena what's going on, it will only bring up feelings I need to shut down. Instead, I watch my breath crystallize in the air in front of me to avoid looking at her and then focus on the glittering city lights. "I'm fine. Just needed the fresh air."

"Oh, no, you don't. You don't get to play that game with me, Archie. Jessica Sims may not know you well enough to see what's going on, but I do. Whatever went down between you and Blaire was personal. You don't walk away from something looking like that unless you love the person."

I still and turn to face her, my hands at my sides. With a sigh, I raise them, palms up. "So what if I do love her? I can't do anything about it."

Athena scoffs and rolls her eyes in the classic move that always gets her in so much trouble with Mom and Dad. "There's nothing you can do? Why are you proposing to that girl tonight and marrying her when you're in love with Blaire?

I grit my teeth and clench my fists. "You know why. Don't act like you don't."

She points back toward the party. "Don't do something stupid for those people in there."

"Grandmother, Grandfather, Mom, and Dad have to die eventually. I just have to wait it out."

"Jesus!" She snorts and shakes her head. "That's a really healthy way to look at things. Let's just count down the days until they kick the bucket, and I can finally be with someone I actually give a shit about."

"That's not fair. I care about Jessica."

"How can you possibly know that? You barely know *her*."

I shove my hands back through my hair, squeeze my eyes shut, and let my head fall back. "She's a sweet girl, Athena. She's fitting into our party and doing an amazing job already. She's exactly what this family and I need right now."

"Wow. You're more messed up than I thought. Here I had hoped that what happened with Artie may have taught you something."

I drop my hands and turn to face her. "I don't want to abandon the family to go live on the beach, Athena. That may be exactly what Artie wants, but you know I always wanted this company. Don't hate me for wanting to have it."

"That's where you're wrong. There is another way —Blaire."

Just her name is enough to tighten the vise around my chest. "I wish it were that simple, but it just…isn't. She doesn't fit into this world."

One of Athena's eyebrows wings up. "She doesn't?"

"She isn't a Warren!"

"That's a good thing, Archie. You of all people should know that." She releases a deep sigh and closes the distance between us, glancing back over her shoulder to make sure no one can hear us. "I understand wanting to protect her from the bullshit that comes with our family, but there's another option."

"Yeah? What's that?"

"Make her one and teach her how to do it. Teach her how to be exactly what you need, not what Grandfather, or Grandmother, or Mother or Father want for you."

"After the conversation I just had with her, it's too late for that, Athena." I turn to walk away from her before she can argue with me further. I'll get my jacket from her later after I have a few dozen more drinks.

I can't discuss this anymore. Not with Athena. Not with Blaire. Not with anyone. This is a losing battle over a moot point. I'll marry Jessica one week from today and make her a Warren. It's the only way.

BLAIRE

It takes a good ten minutes for me to shift from my spot in the middle of the hallway, surrounded by the broken glass at my feet. The conversation with Archie has left me numb and unable to move, practically unable to breathe.

I'm going to have to find a new job. Build a new life somewhere far away from Warren Enterprises and Archimedes Warren. But first, I suck in a deep breath and force my feet to carry me back toward the party. I have to make it through tonight, and I have to finish the wedding plans to ensure Archie's marriage ceremony goes off without a hitch.

Because I'm his assistant, after all, and the man needs to be married. He made himself very clear on that.

"Blaire, darling?" The soft, older feminine voice startles me as I reach the entry back into the party, and I turn to face Ruby Warren.

The matriarch of the family has always brought mixed reviews from those who have met her and heard stories, but during our few interactions when she's come into the offices, she's always been very pleasant with me.

I force a smile I don't feel and nod toward her. "Hello, Mrs. Warren."

She slips her arm through mine, the beads of her Swarovski-encrusted dress rubbing against my sensitive, bare skin. "Let's have a chat."

"A chat?"

The older woman doesn't answer me, just leads me toward the staircase up to the US Presidents exhibit.

I glance over my shoulder at the closed sign. "Are we supposed to be going up here?"

She waves her free hand dismissively. "You really think anyone will stop me?"

A slight giggle escapes my lips despite feeling devastated. "You're right."

No one would stop a Warren. Especially on this night, during their big party.

We reach the top of the stairwell, and she slowly leads me into the gallery containing historical items from different presidencies. She stops in front of the Kennedy portion and lets out a long sigh. "Poor family."

"Did you know them?"

She glances over at me with her pale, old blue eyes twinkling. "Close friends, actually. But I swear, they're cursed. Much the way the Warrens are."

The Warrens...cursed?

I turn to look at her again. "What do you mean?"

Her lips press into a thin line, and she pats my arm. "I overheard a little bit of your disagreement with Archie tonight."

Shit.

I wince and look around for avenues of escape.

She just pats my arm again. "Don't be so worried, Blaire."

"I'm so sorry that happened at the party in public."

Her bony, frail hand waves dismissively. "Oh, honey. That's not why I wanted to talk to you."

"Then, why did you?"

She points to a picture of Jackie O, and a soft smile curls her lips. "She was a beautiful and wonderful woman. And she loved John fiercely. Much the way you do Archie."

Apparently, she overheard one very important part of my conversation with him.

"I know it's inappropriate, ma'am. I'm his assistant..."

She holds up a hand to stop me. "Bearing the Warren name means bearing all the weight that comes with it. That was too much for Artemis, and he caved under the pressure. I saw it coming long before he reconnected with Penelope, and he's recently confirmed for me that he had planned to resign from his position as CEO and open his own law firm before he found out he was a father."

"Wow. I didn't know that. I just assumed it was all because of Penelope and Max."

She smiles softly and shakes her head. "The thing is, Archie has always been more driven than Artemis. Artemis excelled at everything easily, but he didn't have a passion for it. It was always easy for him to do what was expected. On the other hand, Archimedes had to fight and claw his way to the top of his class and the top of Warren Enterprises. And now that it's within his reach, he's afraid to do anything that might jeopardize it. Like giving in to his true feelings for you."

It isn't anything I don't already know. Archimedes has always been very clear about his priorities, and I've witnessed how hard he works—coming in early and staying late.

His life isn't mine.

I blink away the impending tears and offer Mrs. Warren a sad smile. "I understand why it can't happen. I'm not meant to be with Archie. I am not Warren material."

She jerks back and turns, finally releasing my arm and stepping in front of me. The wrinkles around her eyes and lips pucker as she stares me down. "You just confronted him and called him out on his bullshit at our annual party surrounded by 'Warren people.' If anyone is strong enough to be a Warren, it's you."

Her words tug at my already broken heart, threatening to make me fall apart completely.

I squeeze my eyes closed and shake my head. When I reopen my eyes, a single tear escapes. "I'm not. But Jessica Sims is. Look at her tonight, the way she's on Archie's arm talking to these people."

Mrs. Warren releases a sigh. "She's a very sweet girl. I'll give her that much. But there's no spark between them. Not like with you. I can feel the tension when you and Archie are in the same room. Like two magnets trying to fight against the pull." She places a gentle hand on my arm. "You did the right thing by confronting him tonight. I just hope that my damn grandson comes to his senses and chooses the right woman."

"It's too late for that."

She shakes her head, her white hair bouncing. "It's not. And know that you have Athena and me in your corner."

I raise an eyebrow at her. "Really?"

She grins and places a hand against my lower back to lead me farther into the exhibit. "Warren women can recognize one of their own. At least, the smart ones of us. Sometimes, it's the men who have trouble."

CHAPTER 20

BLAIRE

A fairy-tale wedding at a castle. Today is the day every girl dreams about and waits for. Only…this one is for someone else. I have to watch someone else walk down the aisle to Archie standing, waiting to commit the rest of his life to her.

And I have to do it knowing it's not what he wants. That he's doing it out of some misguided desire to protect me from the Warrens.

It's all such bullshit.

I suck in a deep breath to prevent myself from sobbing again. The last thing I need is everyone seeing me with red, puffy eyes and running makeup. They'd know something was wrong, and I don't think I can play it off as happy tears for my boss.

I also don't know if I'll be able to make it through the ceremony. I'll have to bail before it starts. Once I make sure everything is in order, of course. Because one thing I refuse to do is fail at my job.

No matter what happened between Archie and me, I committed to getting this wedding done and ensuring it goes off without a hitch. And even through the tears and heartache, I'll complete that task.

I glance at my checklist.

Perfect venue. Check. Belvedere Castle is literally a dream location. The one I've had in my head since I was a little girl and Dad used to bring me to the park for picnics. We would sit and stare up at the castle and watch wedding parties have their pictures taken, and I could see myself there with my future husband smiling at me.

Dress. Check. I turn and glance at the beautiful gown hanging behind me in the ready room given to us at the castle. Jessica picked a stunning gown. Actually, it's exactly what I pictured for myself. Elegant and simple. Athena dropped it off earlier.

Tears well in my eyes again, and I have to turn away before I completely lose my grip on myself.

Flowers. Check. The florist is just putting the finishing touches on the arrangements on either side of the aisle that Jessica will walk down, and the boutonnieres are already in the groom's ready room. My eyes drift to the bouquet. Absolutely perfect, just like I knew it would be.

Wedding party. Check. Athena and Artemis are already here somewhere—both checked in with me via text message this morning. And Jessica's bridesmaids will be arriving with her in the limo.

Officiant. Check. Judge Allenson, one of the Warrens' oldest friends and a federal circuit court judge, is here and ready to go.

That only leaves two more items on the list.

The groom.

I don't have the strength to go searching for him to make sure he has everything he needs. If the office hadn't been closed during this week between the Christmas Eve party and the wedding today, and if I hadn't been taking care of all the wedding planning on my own without having to see him, I don't think I could've handled it. I'm going to assume he's here and ready to go without seeing him. I'm sure someone will come in here screaming bloody murder if there is some issue with him.

The bride. She will be arriving soon. She opted to get ready at the Four Seasons hotel, where they'll be spending their first evening as husband and wife and presumably… consummating the marriage. Just thinking about it makes bile burn up my throat, and I have to swallow it back to keep from retching.

I thought I could do this. I thought I could handle doing this, doing my *job* and staying detached…but I was so wrong.

So damn wrong.

This is a nightmare I may never wake up from.

The door flies open, and Athena buzzes in—hair and makeup already perfectly done and her dark emerald green bridesmaid's dress hugging her perfectly. "There you are." She hustles over to me, grabs my arm, and ushers me across the room toward the dreaded dress. "I need you to just throw this on."

"What?"

She waves her hand in a circular motion. "We don't have much time."

"What the hell's going on?"

"We need to do a few quick alterations, and you and Jessica are the same size."

"We are?"

How is that even possible?

Jessica is tiny, and on top of the height difference, she's considerably smaller than I am.

Athena just waves me off and smiles. "Yes, I double-checked. The seamstress will be here any minute. Please?"

I grit my teeth and nod. "I'll do it."

Jessica deserves to have her dream wedding, even if I can't have mine. I won't get in the way of that. Athena helps me get into the dress, and just as Athena promised, the dress fits me like a glove, almost like it was made to my measurements exactly. I turn to face the floor-to-ceiling mirror in the room. My breath catches, and tears well in my eyes that have somehow managed to maintain most of the makeup I put on this morning.

"Wow." Athena stands next to me, a grin on her face. "You look stunning in that."

I brush my hand over the silky fabric and force a smile. "Jessica will, too." I glance back toward the door. "Where's the seamstress?"

Athena pulls her phone from the tiny bag on her arm. "Oh!"

"What?"

She narrows her eyes on the screen. "Artemis says the judge wants to do a quick run-through of the ceremony before the guests all arrive to make sure everybody knows what they're doing because we didn't have time for a formal rehearsal."

"I made very sure everybody knows where they're supposed to be and when."

"I know," she waves me off, "the judge is just being meticulous. Come with me." She grabs my hand and drags me toward the door, but I plant my feet.

"What are you doing?"

"We need someone to be the bride."

I glance down at the dress. "No. I can't go out there in her dress."

"It'll only take a minute. I promise. Do it for Archie."

Do it for Archie...

Her words tug at my bruised heart, and I relent and let her drag me from the room across the large entryway of the castle and to the vast, high-ceilinged room where the ceremony is supposed to take place.

Soft piano music hits my ears. This must be a full-on rehearsal. Athena squeezes my hand and pulls me to a stop outside the door.

She takes both my hands in hers and squeezes them. "Blaire, remember the day I was in the office and you had the stack of all the applications?"

I nod slowly.

What does this have to do with the wedding rehearsal?

"Well," humor dances in her blue eyes, "I told you to throw away all the good ones."

"What?"

She gives me a guilty little half-smile. "I figured that if I only let through the ones I thought would be bad for Archie that he could see what was right in front of him instead."

I let out a deep sigh and blink away tears. "You were wrong."

She squeezes my hand again and shakes her head. "No, I wasn't."

"What are you—"

Before I can finish my question, Athena drags me in front of the open door, and I lose my ability to speak.

ARCHIMEDES

Blaire has never looked more confused.

Or more beautiful.

The second she stepped into the doorway and I saw her,

GWYN MCNAMEE & CHRISTY ANDERSON

all the air rushed from my lungs. And now, with her eyes locked on mine, standing at the altar, I have to reach up and swipe under my eyes to keep the tears from falling.

I slowly descend the steps and walk down the aisle with the nearly empty chairs on either side.

Blaire's best friend, Brandy, leans toward me. "Go get her!"

I flash her a grin and continue making my way back to Blaire. If it hadn't been for Brandy's help, I'm not so sure we would've even been able to pull this off. But once I realized what an idiot I was being, and after a very heartfelt chat with Grandmother, I knew what I had to do—I had to marry the right woman.

The stubbornness that was keeping me from acknowledging what I needed to do was asinine, and I was ready to spend the rest of my life with a woman I barely knew, who I certainly didn't love, all to fit some mold established by the very people who have made my life a living hell in so many ways.

Christ, I was so stupid.

Prepared to do that when this woman was offering me everything.

I stop in front of Blaire, and her jaw opens and closes, but she doesn't say anything. "I know you're probably really confused right now, Blaire."

She nods slowly. "Yeah, you could say that."

Two more steps bring me to her, and I pull her hands into mine. "I'm doing what I should've done weeks ago." I drop down onto one knee. "Marry me, Blaire."

Her eyes widen. "What?" She scans the faces in the room. "What about Jessica?"

I sigh and glance at Athena, where she stands behind Blaire. "I talked to her, and I told her the truth—that my heart belongs to you. She was upset, understandably, but she said she'd rather have me marry for love."

Blaire's breath hitches, and tears well in her eyes.

I squeeze her hands tightly. "It's a word I never thought I'd say. A word I wasn't sure I would ever understand. But after our talk at the party, and in the hours and days since, it's become abundantly clear to me that I could never be happy with Jessica. Not when my heart belongs to you. So, marry me, Blaire. This is the wedding you wanted, isn't it?"

Please let me be right about this.

I glance back at Brandy.

"Brandy told me what you been doing—using your own wedding plans." I shake my head and pull her hand to my lips to kiss it. "Only you would be so selfless as to plan your dream wedding for someone else."

The perfect day planned for another woman. And she never complained once. She went ahead with all that needed to be done, even after the fiasco on Christmas Eve.

I brush my hand over her dress. "I had this made for you based on a photo Brandy gave me from your book. I hope it's right. I wanted everything to be perfect." I take a shaky breath, one that gives away the nerves running through my body in this moment. "I thought if it was perfect, there might be a chance you'd forgive what a fool I've been and say yes. So, please, Blaire, become my Mrs. Warren. Help me navigate all the bullshit that comes with being part of this family. Because I need a partner I can trust and who understands. Someone who will stand up to me and my mother and father—"

Her eyes widen again, and she shakes her head. "Oh, God, what about your parents?"

I push to my feet and step up to her until my chest brushes against hers and I can take her face between my palms. "I don't care. Even if the trust had some sort of stipulation that meant choosing you would lose me the company, I would *still* be marrying you. Because I love you."

She struggles for words again, when there is really only one I want to hear. "Archie, you know how I feel about you, but—"

"No *but*. There's absolutely nothing stopping us. Nothing standing in our way except ourselves. We have the perfect venue," I wave a hand around, "your best friend is here to be your maid of honor. We have an officiant, my brother and sister, and a beautiful reception. I don't need anything or anyone else. This wedding is for *us,* not the hundreds of people I invited out of obligation. *And* I made it clear that my parents weren't to be admitted if they showed up here."

"You forgot to warn them about me, though." Grandmother steps up next to Athena and grins at me.

"Hello, Grandmother."

Blaire glances at her with concern etched on her beautiful face.

Grandmother winks. "I told you he would come to his senses eventually. Have you agreed to marry this idiot yet?"

I chuckle and shake my head. "No, she hasn't."

She waves a hand. "Well, get on with it."

Blaire grins and shakes her head. "This is all so insane."

I lean in and drop my forehead against hers. "It is, but so is my life. And I need you in it. Please marry me." I pull back and look into her emerald eyes, ones I hope I get to gaze into for the rest of my life.

She leans in and presses a soft kiss to my lips. "Yes. I'll marry you."

They're the sweetest words I've ever heard, and the rush of relief that floods my body has me dragging her against me. "I know I'm supposed to wait until you say 'I do' but—" I press my lips to hers in a hard, demanding kiss—one that is probably inappropriate in front of everyone, yet she wraps her arms around my neck and responds to me, her lips moving against mine almost desperately.

When I finally drag myself away, I take her hand in mine. "We'll walk down the aisle together."

She grins up at me. "Not very traditional."

"I don't think anything about this wedding is."

Her laugh floats through the room, and the sound of her pure joy fills my chest with the warmth it's been missing for the last week.

"That's true."

Athena and Grandmother take their seats at the front, and Artemis and Brandy smile at us from either side of the altar. The piano starts up, and we walk down the aisle hand in hand to take our places in front of Judge Allenson.

He smiles at us. "We're gathered here today to join Archimedes Warren and Blaire Hall in marriage. Given the circumstances…" he flashes a smile and chuckles, "we're just going to wing it."

Everyone laughs, and I squeeze Blaire's hand, refusing to let it go for fear she might bolt out of here.

The judge inclines his head toward me. "Archimedes, are you ready to say your vows?"

I clear my throat and turn to face Blaire, pulling both her hands in mine. "Blaire. There's not much I can say that you don't already know. I never thought you and I would ever happen, and when we did, it was like a light in my life when I hadn't even known I'd been living in darkness."

Tears well in her eyes, and I pull one hand from hers to reach up and brush them away with my thumb.

"I'm sorry I put you through so much to get here and was such an idiot. And I'm sure I'm going to be an idiot again—many, many times over what I hope is our very long marriage."

She giggles and nods her agreement.

"But I promise to always come home to you at night and that you will always be the one who holds my heart. I love you." I choke back the sob threatening to climb up my throat and swallow. "And I'm so happy you're going to be my wife."

Blaire stares up at me, and I don't even bother to try to catch the tears now flowing in earnest from her eyes.

Judge Allenson inclines his head toward her. "Blaire, I know you really haven't had much time to prepare, but are you ready to say your vows?"

She nods and sucks in a deep breath before glancing at the few people in the chairs. "Well, today has certainly been full of surprises." Her gaze returns to mine, and she grins at me. "I don't know how you managed to pull this off. The last place I expected to be was standing on this altar with you today. But I'm so glad you finally came to your senses."

I chuckle and squeeze her hand.

"I may not be the typical Warren bride, but like your grandmother said the other night, I might be exactly what the Warrens need. And you're *definitely* what I need. So, I promise to always come home to you and that you'll always hold my heart, too."

"Do you have the rings?"

The judge's question drags my attention away from Blaire, and Artemis steps forward and hands them to him. It would have been nice to have Penelope and Max here for the ceremony, but with her being in the third trimester and a cold that's been plaguing Max the last week, travelling with Artie just wasn't in the cards.

I take the solitaire diamond and matching wedding band and slip them onto Blaire's finger. "This was my grandmother's. She wanted you to have it."

Blaire flights back a sob and glances at Grandmother.

The judge hands Blaire my simple white gold band, and she slides it on my finger. Some men might feel like getting married and wearing one of these is a burden. Something that holds you back, but to me, it feels like finally being complete.

Judge Allenson grins and raises his arms. "Without further ado, I now pronounce you husband and wife. You may kiss your bride."

I take her face in my palms and tilt it up toward me. "I love you, Mrs. Warren."

"I love you, Mister Warren."

"I guess Christmas miracles really can happen."

She smiles up at me, true happiness lighting her face. "I always believed they could."

And then her lips find mine, and everything around us melts away like the snow gently falling over the castle in Central Park.

EPILOGUE

TWO MONTHS LATER

BLAIRE

I *love it here.*

Standing in the sands of Cape Harmony, the cool February wind blowing in off the ocean, it reminds me of that day just a few short months ago when I left Archie with a face full of smashed cake and my broken heart at his feet.

There will be cake today, too, but we'll be eating this one under much happier circumstances—Athena's birthday.

It was the perfect excuse to take a much-needed break and for all of us to come to meet Artie's and Pen's newest addition, Persephone Maia Warren.

Born just a few weeks ago, she's already the spitting image of her beautiful mother. And I've fallen in love with them both so fast.

I look down where the little bundle of joy is nestled asleep in the crook of my arm and smile.

None of this would have been possible if it hadn't been for Athena. That beautiful, meddling girl made sure I got my fairy-tale wedding in Central Park that snowy day.

I am married to Archimedes Warren. I am Mrs. Blaire Warren.

It's still sometimes hard to wrap my head around. It was quite a wild ride, and I wouldn't change a single second of our story.

Well, maybe a chapter or two.

Definitely nothing *after* the wedding,

Flying off on a surprise honeymoon was as unexpected as the wedding itself. Archie refused to reveal the location. And when we landed, I knew why.

North Pole, Alaska.

Not exactly the tropical paradise most people explore for their honeymoon, but then, Artie never does anything normal. And it was the best location he could have chosen because it showed just how much he really *cared.*

I had only mentioned saving up for the trip in passing to him that night we spent together. So ending up there as a couple after a surprise wedding was like the icing on the cake. The fact that he remembered meant more to me than the actual trip that I had been saving up for and planning to take myself.

And in typical Archie fashion, he gave me the most amazing wedding gift upon our return to New York—a new snow globe for my collection.

I'm beginning to think he enjoys them almost as much as I do.

Though this one was special—perfect little figure replicas of us, in Central Park on our wedding day. A beautiful moment down to every last detail, perfectly frozen in time. The groom lifting the bride off her feet in an embrace.

I still get teary-eyed every time I think about it. But I'm not going to cry standing on this beautiful beach with this baby in my arms. Archie and Artie chase Max across the sand, and their laughter is contagious. Max flings his arms out wide like he is flying.

This moment is the picture of bliss.

Max looks like he could be his Uncle Archie's son, and seeing him while holding this little one makes me dream of what our little angel will look like.

Will he or she look like me with red hair and green eyes or like Archie with inky hair and ocean eyes?

Maybe a mix of both.

Seeing him with Max only makes it more clear how badly we both want a child. Even though we've been trying to conceive in the two months since the wedding, it had nothing to do with the trust requirements and everything to do with our own desire to start a family.

Archie pushes Artie out of his way to scoop up Max and twirls him around in the air. All this joy and laughter makes everything we went through, every wonderful, sometimes painful moment, worth it in the end.

Penelope steps up next to me and watches the boys. "It's time for cake. Let me take her. Your arms need a break by now."

I kiss baby Persephone's forehead, drinking in that new baby scent as I watch my husband stroll across the sand toward me.

"You're going to be a great mom, Blaire. I just know it." Pen smiles as I slide the baby over to her waiting arms.

"You think?"

I hope so. Luckily, Archie seems to be a natural. I practically have to fight him to get Persephone out of his arms.

"I know so. Help me get the birthday candles lit?" She turns and starts up the beach toward her house.

"Yeah, need me to hold the baby while you light the candles?"

I follow behind her but turn back for one last look at Archie. The wind whips his dark hair, and he flashes me an infectious smile and mouths *I love you.*

In the end, the man who broke my heart held all of the delicate pieces in his hands and stitched them back together. He made it stronger, more whole than it ever was before.

ARCHIMEDES

I recline in the chair on the back porch of Artie's beach house and glance over at him.

His eyes meet mine, and he grins. "Are you happy?"

It's the exact question I once asked him sitting on this same porch after he chose to give up everything I just almost ruined my life to have.

I don't even need to think of my response. "Fuck, yes. I've never been happier."

I chuckle, but it's the damn truth.

I'm happier than I have ever been.

When I think back to last summer, watching with a bit of jealousy as Artie chased Max around in the sand, I know I wanted that for myself. That happiness, that freedom from the Warren name, that love. But I wanted the company, my legacy, just as much.

"Cheers." He stretches his bottle of beer out, and I tap mine to his.

"Cheers." I take a swig and enjoy the waves crashing against the shore.

This visit is definitely different than last summer. I have a wife this time, and sooner rather than later, I'll return here with a child of my own.

The door slides open, and Penelope comes out to join us. "Guys, we're getting the cake ready. Artie, can you round up Athena and bring her inside in just a few? She's out strolling the beach." Pen kisses Art on his cheek before she heads back inside.

"You're pussy whipped," I taunt.

He just laughs. "Absolutely. Just like you."

Proudly so.

We both stand, and he heads down the steps to the beach in search of Athena while I head inside to find Blaire. I push open the glass door and spot her digging in the top drawer of the buffet table in the dining room.

I close the distance, eager to get my hands on her. "Hello, wife." I slide my arms around Blaire's waist from behind and nestle my lips into the crook of her neck, one of my favorite spots to kiss.

She smells like sea and air, and I inhale her scent, drinking in this moment.

"Mmm. Hello, husband."

I'll never get tired of hearing that word spill from her beautiful lips. I never thought I'd have this—her. It was a long road, and boy, was I a stubborn fool. But we got here.

Thank God, we made it. For that, for her, I will be eternally grateful.

I spin her within the cage of my arms, so she faces me. "You ready to get out of here?" I waggle my eyebrows. "We've got babies to make."

She chuckles and playfully slaps at my chest. "Stop it. We are about to have cake. I need to get the candles lit."

Boring.

I'd much rather be making babies.

She pecks my lips, and I watch as her gorgeous ass sways as she heads back toward the kitchen to help Pen.

I exhale a contented breath. I love this place, and not just because Artie and Pen and the kids are here.

Despite all the Warren drama, this beach and this town still hold a lot of good memories. Coming here growing up in the summers and being at Mom and Dad's place a few miles up the road were amazing times. I'm not going to let my resentment of them or what they try to force on me ruin this place. Plus, Blaire loves it, and I hope she loves the little house we rented on the beach next door because I just bought it for us.

We need this. A place to get out of the city, see Archie and his family, and, hopefully, vacation with our own growing one.

"The birthday girl has arrived." Athena enters through the back door, and Artie moves past her to go to the kitchen.

"Hey, sis." I tip my beer toward her. "Where'd you disappear to?"

She walks toward me and punches me in the arm, hard.

"Ouch, damn it. What the hell was that for?" I rub the spot that now throbs.

She got me good.

"You're a wuss. It's all your fault!" She laughs, but the annoyed look on her face worries me.

"What's going on?" I lean against the buffet and wait for her answer, still rubbing my arm.

"I was strolling along the beach, enjoying my day, and then Mother called." She rolls her eyes. "I knew I shouldn't have answered, but it is my birthday, and I thought it was rude to ignore the woman who brought me into this world, you know?"

I wait for her to continue. Her question wasn't really a question. I can already tell this call did not go well.

"So, of course, she only calls to inform me that now you and Art have settled down, it's high time I get myself and my priorities in line. She said that I have had enough idle time. So, thanks. You basically just ruined my life with your disgusting happiness."

She rolls her eyes, laughs, and bumps her shoulder into my arm.

"There better be cake. And booze. Mostly booze."

I follow her into the kitchen, listen to a disgustingly off-key rendition of "Happy Birthday," and then we all settle out onto the porch to eat our cake.

"Cake and beer, an interesting combination." Blaire giggles from where she perches on my knee, eating her dessert.

"Food for the gods." I take a sip of beer and slide it back onto the side table with the rest of my uneaten cake.

I grab Blaire's waist and adjust her more comfortably across my lap. "Better?"

"Yes, thank you. Want a bite?" She offers me the fork.

"You sure you don't want to smash it into my face?"

She giggles, and I open my mouth as she slides the confection across my lips. "Not today."

With my wife on my lap and my family gathered around me, I stare off at the ocean rising and swelling.

This is contentment.

Somehow, everything has worked out in my favor, and I couldn't be happier or more grateful than I am in this moment.

I twirl my fingers around one of Blaire's curls and give it a tug. She turns, and I take the opportunity to palm her cheek and to kiss her.

"Eww, yuck." Max groans.

I can't help but laugh as I kiss Blaire, one last peck to the lips. "One day, little man, you'll see just how not gross kissing is."

"Archie," Artemis warns, and we all share a laugh at Max's expense.

Only a few months ago, I thought this was impossible.

Marrying a woman I actually love.

Marrying a woman who loves me for me. Not my name, not who I am or what my name brings to the table.

Blaire couldn't care less about my money—our money. And I got the other thing I wanted: I get to run the company.

Though, that part is a little less important to me now.

My desire to protect her goodness from the monster the Warrens can be and this life and the fear that all of this would somehow change her, eat her up, has abated. I should have known that nothing can make Blaire do anything she doesn't want to do.

She's loyal, strong, courageous, and honorable. That will never change. That's who Blaire Warren is. She's everything wonderful, just like she has always been. Instead of being dulled by the Warren way of life, she shimmers like freshly fallen snow with her love for me. And me, I'm a lucky bastard because I get to love her.

And that love makes me the wealthiest man in the world.

We hope you enjoyed *Holiday Bridal Wave.*

Want more from the Warren family?

You can preorder book three, *Holiday Fake Date*, Athena's story, coming in November 2021:
www.books2read.com/HolidayFakeDate

If you haven't already read Artemis' story, *Holiday Terminal*, grab your copy now: www. books2read.com/HolidayTerminal

ABOUT THE AUTHOR - GWYN MCNAMEE

Gwyn McNamee is an attorney, writer, wife, and mother (to one human baby and two fur babies). Originally from the Midwest, Gwyn relocated to her husband's home town of Las Vegas in 2015 and is enjoying her respite from the cold and snow. Gwyn has been writing down her crazy stories and ideas for years and finally decided to share them with the world. She loves to write stories with a bit of suspense and action mingled with romance and heat.

When she isn't either writing or voraciously devouring any books she can get her hands on, Gwyn is busy adding to her tattoo collection, golfing, and stirring up trouble with her perfect mix of sweetness and sarcasm (usually while wearing heels).

Gwyn loves to hear from her readers.
Here is where you can find her:
Facebook:
https://www.facebook.com/AuthorGwynMcNamee/
Twitter:
https://twitter.com/GwynMcNamee
Instagram:
https://www.instagram.com/gwynmcnamee
Bookbub:
https://www.bookbub.com/authors/gwyn-mcnamee
FB Reader Group:
https://www.facebook.com/groups/1667380963540655/

Website:
https://www.gwynmcnamee.com

AVAILABLE NOW AT ALL RETAILERS:

books2read.com/SquallLine

Rogue Wave (Book Two)

CUTTER

Complete the mission.

It's what I was trained to do—no matter what.

But when things go to shit right in front of me, my objective gets compromised by a set of fathomless amber eyes.

This isn't a woman's world.

Yet, Valentina refuses to see how dangerous the course she's plotted really is.

How dangerous I am.

VALENTINA

The man who saved my life is just as lethal as the one trying to take it.

Maybe even more.

While he may have rescued me, in the end,

Cutter is my enemy.

The one intent on destroying everything I've striven for.

But the scars of his past draw me closer even though I know I should move away.

Cutter and Valentina.

Anger and desire.

Fight and surrender.

This wave may drag them both under...

AVAILABLE AT ALL RETAILERS:

Safe Harbor (Book Three)

PREACHER

When it comes to firewalls, no one gets

through my defenses.

For the past five years, protecting this band of f-ed up brothers has been my mission.

But Everly pulls me from my cave and does the one thing no one else ever has...

She makes me believe there's a life outside the world

on my screens.

Too bad actions have consequences, ones that threaten everything and everyone around me.

Including the beautiful tattoo artist who has managed to etch herself onto my heart.

EVERLY

The emotional upheaval of the last six months would be enough to break anyone.

And I can already feel myself cracking.

A tall, sexy, tattooed bad boy is the last thing I need thrown into the mix.

All I want is to keep my head down and pour my pain

into my art.

But Preacher walks into my life and offers me safety in a world where I thought there was none.

Until our pasts finally catch up with us...

Preacher and Everly.

Fear and loss.

Hope and heartbreak.

This harbor may be their salvation.

AVAILABLE AT ALL RETAILERS:

books2read.com/SafeHarbor

Anchor Point (Book Four)

ELIJAH

Life outside the walls of my prison cell is far harder than the time I did inside.

There, I had my misery to keep me company.

Out here, I'm forced to face the reality of

everything I've lost.

Nothing can repair the gaping hole in my chest.

Yet, a broken woman wrapped in chains threatens to unravel the tangle of excuses I use to keep everyone

at arm's length.

But letting Evangeline into my world means exposing her to the real threat.

Me.

And all the terrible things that come along with that.

EVANGELINE

Taken.

Enslaved.

To be sold to the highest bidder.

The monsters who stole me away from my life

have no conscience.

I'm not so sure the man who rescues me is any different.

He's an ex-con and a pirate— not to be trusted.

But the dark veil of anguish that shrouds him can't hide the truth of who he is at his core.

Elijah isn't the enemy.

He may be broken and tormented…

And exactly what I need.

Elijah and Evangeline.

Agony and regret.

Faith and acceptance.

This anchor may pull them both down...

AVAILABLE AT ALL RETAILERS:

books2read.com/AnchorPoint

Dark Tide (Book Five)

RION

There is no black and white in this life.

The line between right and wrong blurs.

I'm constantly crossing it.

Saving a life is just as easy as taking one.

And I'm damn good at both.

Finding a woman who can survive in this world was never on the radar.

But Gabriella pulls me from the bottom of a bottle and touches me in a way no one else can.

Too bad secrets and lies have a way of catching up with everyone.

GABRIELLA

How did I end up here, slinging drinks at a dive bar in the middle of nowhere?

The choices that brought me to this were never even a glimmer of possibility only a few years ago.

How things can change so fast…

And now, my path puts me on a collision course with Orion Gates.

His bigger-than-life size and personality should be a warning.

The profession he's chosen should be the ultimate final straw.

But instead, I find myself unable to resist his pull.

A decision that could lead to the end of all of us.

Rion and Gabriella.

Lust and lies.

Betrayal and ruin.

This tide may drown everyone…

AVAILABLE AT ALL RETAILERS:

books2read.com/DarkTide

The Hawke Family Series

Savage Collision **(The Hawke Family - Book One)**

He's everything she didn't know she wanted. She's everything he thought he could never have.

The last thing I expect when I walk into The Hawkeye Club is to fall head over heels in lust. It's supposed to be a rescue mission. I have to get my baby sister off the pole, into some clothes, and out of the grasp of the pussy peddler who somehow manipulated her into stripping. But the moment I see Savage Hawke and verbally spar with him, my ability to remain rational flies out the window and my libido takes center stage. I've never wanted a relationship—my time is better spent focusing on taking down the scum running this city —but what I want and what I need are apparently two different things.

Danika Eriksson storms into my office in her high heels and on her high horse. Her holier-than-thou attitude and accusations should offend me, but instead, I can't get her out of my head or my heart. Her incomparable drive, take-no prisoners attitude, and blatant honesty captivate me and hold me prisoner. I should steer clear, but my self-preservation instinct is apparently dead—which is exactly what our relationship will be once she knows everything. It's only a matter of time.

The truth doesn't always set you free. Sometimes, it just royally screws you.

AVAILABLE NOW AT ALL RETAILERS:

books2read.com/SavageCollision

Tortured Skye (The Hawke Family - Book Two)

She's always been off-limits. He's always just out of reach.

Falling in love with Gabe Anderson was as easy as breathing. Fighting my feelings for my brother's best friend was agonizingly hard. I never imagined giving in to my desire for him would cause such a destructive ripple effect. That kiss was my grasp at a lifeline— something, anything to hold me steady in my crumbling life. Now, I have to suffer with the fallout while trying to convince him it's all worth the consequences.

Guilt overwhelms me—over what I've done, the lives I've taken, and more than anything, over my feelings for Skye Hawke. Craving my best friend's little sister is insanely self-destructive. It never should have happened, but since the moment she kissed me, I haven't been able to get her out of my mind. If I take what I want, I risk losing everything. If I don't, I'll lose her and a piece of myself. The raging storm threatening to rain down on the city is nothing compared to the one that will come from my decision.

Love can be torture, but sometimes, love is the only thing that can save you.

Stone Sober (The Hawke Family - Book Three)

She's innocent and sweet. He's dark and depraved.

Stone Hawke is precisely the kind of man women are warned about — handsome, intelligent, arrogant, and intricately entangled with some dangerous people. I should stay away, but he manages to strip my soul bare with just a look and dominates my thoughts. Bad decisions are in my past. My life is (mostly) on track, even if it is no longer the one to medical school. I can't allow myself to cave to the fierce pull and ardent attraction I feel toward the youngest Hawke.

Nora Eriksson is off-limits, and not just because she's my brother's employee and sister-in-law. Despite the fact she's stripping at The Hawkeye Club, she has an innocent and pure heart. Normally, the only thing that appeals to me about innocence is the opportunity to taint it. But not when it comes to Nora. I can't expose her to the filth permeating my life. There are too many things I can't control, things completely out of my hands. She doesn't deserve any of it, but the power she holds over me is stronger than any addiction.

The hardest battles we fight are often with ourselves, but only through defeating our own demons can we find true peace.

Building Storm (The Hawke Family - Book Four)

She hasn't been living. He's looking for a way to forget it all.

My life went up in flames. All I'm left with is my daughter and ashes. The simple act of breathing is so excruciating, there are days I wish I could stop altogether. So I have no business being at the party, and I definitely shouldn't be in the arms of the handsome stranger. When his lips meet mine, he breathes life into me for the first time since the day the inferno disintegrated my world. But loving again isn't in the cards, and there are even greater dangers to face than trying to keep Landon McCabe out of my heart.

Running is my only option. I have to get away from Chicago and the betrayal that shattered my world. I need a new life-one without attachments. The vibrancy of New Orleans convinces me it's possible to start over. Yet in all the excitement of a new city, it's Storm Hawke's dark, sad beauty that draws me in. She isn't looking for love, and we both need a hot, sweaty release without feelings getting involved. But even the best laid plans fail, and life can leave you burned.

Love can build, and love can destroy. But in the end, love is what raises you from the ashes.

Tainted Saint (The Hawke Family - Book Five)

He's searching for absolution. She wants her happily ever after.

Solomon Clarke goes by Saint, though he's anything but. After lusting for him from afar, the masquerade party affords me the anonymity to pursue that attraction without worrying about the fall-out of hooking-up with the bouncer from the Hawkeye Club. From the second he lays his eyes and hands on me, I'm helpless to resist him. Even burying myself in a dangerous investigation can't erase the memory of our combustible connection and one night together. The only problem... he has no idea who I am.

Caroline Brooks thinks I don't see her watching me, the way her eyes rake over me with appreciation. But I've noticed, and the party is the perfect opportunity to unleash the desire I've kept reined in for so damn long. It also sets off a series of events no one sees coming. Events that leave those I love hurting because of my failures. While the guilt eats away at my soul, Caroline continues to weigh on my heart. That woman may be the death of me, but oh, what a way to go.

Life isn't always clean, and sometimes, it takes a saint to do the dirty work.

AVAILABLE AT ALL RETAILERS:

books2read.com/TaintedSaint

Steele Resolve (The Hawke Family - Book Six)

For one man, power is king. For the other, loyalty reigns.

Mob boss Luca "Steele" Abello isn't just dangerous—he's lethal. A master manipulator, liar, and user, no one should trust a word that comes out of his mouth. Yet, I can't get him out of my head. The time we spent together before I knew his true identity is seared into my brain. His touch. His voice. They haunt my every waking hour and occupy my dreams. So does my guilt. I'm literally sleeping with the enemy and betraying the only family I've ever had. When I come clean, it will be the end of me.

Byron Harris is a distraction I can't afford. I never should have let it go beyond that first night, but I couldn't stay away. Even when I learned who he was, when the *only* option was to end things, I kept going back, risking his life and mine to continue our indiscretion. The truth of what I am could get us both killed, but being with the man who's such an integral part of the Hawke family is even more terrifying. The only people I've ever cared about are on opposing sides, and I'm the rift that could end their friendship forever.

Love is a battlefield isn't just a saying. For some, it's a reality.

AVAILABLE AT ALL RETAILERS:

books2read.com/SteeleResolve

The Deadliest Sin Series (Dark Romance)

WRATH (Book One)

All I see is red.

Blood.

Pain.

Rage.

It consumes me.

The moment he took her, wrath invaded my soul.

I only have one purpose.

End him and take back what's mine.

Love isn't always clean, and wrath is the deadliest sin.

AVAILABLE AT ALL RETAILERS: books2read.com/DeadliestSin1

AFTER WRATH (Book Two)

They took something from me.

Something that can never be replaced.

They destroyed something.

Something that can never be repaired.

Only one thing can appease the burning rage in my soul.

Unleashing my wrath on those responsible.

The Dragon will rise.

Death will reign.

Because wrath is the deadliest sin.

AVAILABLE AT ALL RETAILERS: books2read.com/DeadliestSin2

SURVIVING WRATH (Book Three)

I fled into the night and didn't look back.

I grieved.

I loved.

Then he appears.

Dark.

Dangerous.

I never thought wrath would find me again.

But you can't run from it.

Not when wrath is the deadliest sin

AVAILABLE AT ALL RETAILERS: books2read.com/DeadliestSin3

The Slip Series (Romantic Comedy)

Dickslip (A Scandalous Slip Story #1)

One wardrobe malfunction. Two lives forever changed.

Playing in a star-studded charity basketball game should be fun, and it is, until I literally go balls out to show up my arch nemesis. When I dive for the basketball and my junk slips out of my gym shorts, I know my life and career are over. There's no way the network can keep my kids' show on the air after I've exposed myself to millions of people. I don't know how Andy, the new CEO, can go to bat for me with such passion. I also never anticipate how hot she looks in a pair of high heels.

Rafe's dickslip has made my new job even more stressful. It's hard enough being a woman in a man's world without dealing with sex organs being publicly displayed when someone is representing the company. But he's an asset to the network, not to mention hot as hell. I can barely keep my eyes off him or his crotch during our meetings. Defending him to the board puts my ass on the line as much as his, but it's worth it. So is risking my job to fulfill the fantasies I've had about him since he first set foot in my office.

Things may have started out bad, but... some accidents have happy endings.

AVAILABLE NOW AT ALL RETAILERS:

www.Books2read.com/Dickslip

Nipslip (A Scandalous Slip Story #2)

One nipple. A world of problems.

I own the runway. Until my nipple pops out of my dress during New York Fashion Week and it suddenly owns me. Being called a worthless gutter slut by a fuming designer is the least of my problems. My career is swirling around the toilet like the other models' lunches. Until smoking hot Tate Decker steps in with a crazy idea about how his magazine can maybe salvage my livelihood.

It's less than two feet in front of me. Perfect and perky and pink. And the woman it's attached to looks absolutely horrified. I need to help her, and not just because she's beautiful and has a perfect rack. Using my position in the industry to expose the volatile nature of our business puts my career in jeopardy in an attempt to save Riley's. I'm willing to risk that, but falling for her isn't part of the plan.

When love and tits are involved... Things can get slippery.

AVAILABLE NOW AT ALL RETAILERS:

www.Books2read.com/Nipslip

Beaver Blunder (A Scandalous Slip Story #3)

One brief mistake. A world of hurt.

No panties. No problem. At least until I slip on the wet floor and go heels over head in front of my colleagues and half the courthouse. Returning to consciousness can't be more awkward, until I find out who my sexy, argumentative, and bossy knight in shining armor really is. My career may not survive my beaver blunder, and my heart might not survive Owen Grant.

Madeline Ryan tumbles into my life on a wave of perfume and public embarrassment. She falls and exposes herself in front of me, and I find myself falling for her despite the fact she fights me every chance she gets. Being a woman in a good ol' boy profession demands a certain brashness, but it definitely has me thinking, maybe litigators shouldn't be lovers.

With stressful jobs and big attitudes, going commando has never been so freeing.

AVAILABLE NOW AT ALL RETAILERS:

www.Books2read.com/BeaverBlunder

ABOUT THE AUTHOR - CHRISTY ANDERSON

Writing with a whole lot of sarcasm and humor, mixed with a bit of Southern charm, Christy Anderson ain't no sweet tea kinda storyteller.

As an author of romance, Christy believes it doesn't always have to be hearts and flowers; sometimes, it is dark and twisted, but romance nonetheless. She mixes terror, revenge, and a sliver of love and hope into stories about family, friends, struggles, blurred lines, and happily-ever-afters.

Christy lives in the beautiful mountains of Eastern Tennessee with her husband and 152 cats (not really, but close), where she enjoys writing one twist at a time.

Web Page (under construction): https://www. christyandersonauthor.com
Facebook: www.facebook.com/Christy-Anderson-Author
Facebook Reader Group: https://www.facebook.com/ groups/461018120762644
Goodreads: www.goodreads.com/christy_anderson
Instagram: Christy_Anderson_Author

OTHER WORKS BY CHRISTY ANDERSON

The Killing Hours

(Dark Romance/Romantic Suspense)

The Hunted **(Book One)**

My heart beats furiously in my chest trying to keep up with the pace
I have set.

I am running as fast as I can but it is pointless.

They will catch me.

I am only delaying the inevitable, postponing my

fate if you will.

I know what will happen when they catch me.

It's the same ending every time.

Still, I push my legs as fast as they will go, my body aches from the
exertion.

I can hear them behind me.

They are closing in.

This is part of a twisted game.

The goal, to catch their Prey.

Me.

I am the prize for the Hunter.

I am the Hunted.

AVAILABLE NOW: books2read.com/TheHuntedCA

❄

Book Club Novellas
(Romantic Comedy)

Glory Hole (Book One)

Typically, I'm not the kind of girl to spy on someone.

Really. I'm not.

So why, you ask, do I have my eye pressed to the wall of my living room,

spying on him through my own private glory hole?

Have you seen Beckett Jameson?

AVAILABLE NOW: books2read.com/GloryHole

Rim Job (Book Two)

You would think going to Las Vegas to celebrate your best friend's wedding would be a great time.

You'd be wrong.I'm the kind of girl who plays by the rules.

Las Vegas is the place where rules go to die.

I have a checklist for my life, an order in which the things on that list are supposed to happen.

So far, all has gone according to plan.

That is, until one fateful night when I meet him.

My list wasn't prepared for him.

Frankly, neither was I.

What happens in Vegas doesn't always stay there.

AVAILABLE NOW: books2read.com/RimJob